THEY CALLED HIM *CUCHILO*—"THE KNIFE"

To give him credit, Kansas was fast. But the Kid moved like a *Pehnane* warrior. As the Colt left leather, its hammer drawn back, the Kid's left hand blurred to slap its barrel outward. Flame ripped from the revolver's muzzle, but the bullet missed the Kid by inches. At almost the same moment, the great blade of the bowie knife sprang from its sheath.

The clipped point raked at and bit deep into Kansas' throat. Blood spurted in the wake of the shining steel and the man stumbled backward. Letting his Colt drop, he turned and collapsed onto a table. Coughing out his lifeblood, he slid from there to the floor. . . .

Books by J. T. Edson

THE NIGHT HAWK
NO FINGER ON THE TRIGGER
THE BAD BUNCH
SLIP GUN
TROUBLED RANGE
THE FASTEST GUN IN TEXAS
THE HIDE AND TALLOW MEN
THE JUSTICE OF COMPANY Z
McCRAW'S INHERITANCE
RAPIDO CLINT
COMANCHE
A MATTER OF HONOR

Renegade

J. T. EDSON

A DELL BOOK

Published by
Dell Publishing
a division of
Bantam Doubleday Dell Publishing Group, Inc.
666 Fifth Avenue
New York, New York 10103

ISBN: 0-440-20964-1

Printed in the United States of America

Published simultaneously in Canada

August 1991

10   9   8   7   6   5   4   3   2   1

RAD

For Jerry "Jesbo" Culley,
Best Plug-Maker and Third Best
Pike Fisherman in Melton Mowbray

1

THE WAR'S OVER, SAILOR

"What're you fixing to do now, Miss Belle?" asked Sam Ysabel, sitting with his back against a wall of the dining room in Bannister's Hotel.

Over the years, Ysabel had made sufficient enemies to render the precaution second nature. He always preferred to have a wall behind him, even when eating in a respectable Brownsville hotel.

"I don't know," Belle Boyd admitted. "What does a spy do when the war's over and she's served on the losing side?"

"You could always go back home," suggested Ysabel's son, having selected a chair that allowed him an uninterrupted view across the table at the hotel's lobby.

"Home!" Belle repeated the word bitterly. "I don't have a home anymore. A bunch of Abolitionists saw to that back in '61."

Tall, slender, although by no means skinny, the girl had coal-black hair cut almost boyishly short. She wore an expensive, stylish, if travel-stained, black jacket and riding skirt, a frilly-bosomed white blouse and dainty, calf-high boots. Beautiful features, with strength of will and intelligence in their lines, displayed little of the concern she might feel for the future. Her voice, with its well-educated Deep South drawl, expressed unspoken anger as she mentioned her loss.

As Belle claimed, she no longer had a home. Not since the night, early in 1861, when Alfred Tollinger and George Barmain had led a mob, consisting of rabidly violent pro-Union fanatics and ordinary drunken rabble in search of a chance to loot and pillage, against her father's plantation. The family and house servants had fought back desperately. However, before the Boyds' "downtrodden and abused" slaves had rallied and helped to drive off the attackers, Belle had been wounded, her parents murdered and the once magnificent mansion destroyed by fire. To escape justice, the leaders of the mob had fled to the North. The start of the War Between the States had prevented their arrest and return to Baton Royale for trial.

Belle's wound had healed in time, but it left her with a deep and lasting desire for revenge and a hatred of the Union's supporters that she had not felt before the attack. The brutal, irresponsible and ill-advised actions of a pair of intellectual fanatics was to cost the North dearly in the years that followed. Wanting to avenge her parents, Belle had sought for a way to do so. Learning that a cousin, Rose Greenhow, intended to organize a spy ring, Belle had offered her services in the hope that the work would bring her into contact with Tollinger and Barmain. Knowing of the girl's unconventional upbringing, Rose had been only too willing to enroll her.

Wanting a son, and learning that his wife could have no more children, Vincent Boyd had insisted on instructing his daughter in several subjects not normally taught to a wealthy Southern girl. By sixteen, she could ride a horse—astride, not sidesaddle —and follow a hound pack as well as any of her fox-hunting male neighbors. At twenty, when the mob had arrived, she was a skilled performer with a dueling sword, a deadly shot with a handgun and had also acquired a thorough knowledge of *savate:* French Creole foot- and fist-boxing.

Belle's lessons in the more usual feminine accomplishments had not been neglected and, but for the raid on her home, she would probably have put aside her masculine skills, taken a husband and lived a conventional life. Instead she made use of her training as a member of the newly formed, but very efficient, Confederate States Secret Service organization.

Not for Belle Boyd the routine and intrigue of making contacts, worming confidences from susceptible males or accumulating information. She had preferred the more active task of delivering her fellow agents' gatherings to their superiors in the organization. Coming and going through the Union Army's lines, she had relied upon disguises, quick wits, riding or fighting skills to avoid cature. Her fame grew and she was given the name "the Rebel Spy" for her efforts in the South's cause.

All through the war, wherever its fortunes carried her, she had looked for Tollinger and Barmain. Rumor had it that they were members of the United States Secret Service, but Belle had failed to locate them. Despite military hostilities having ended, she felt disinclined to forgive or forget what the two men had done to her parents, although she knew that gaining her revenge would not be easy.

Typical of Belle, while unsure of what the future might hold for her, she also wondered how her companions would make out now that peace had returned to the United States. Yet she guessed that her fears on their behalf might be unfounded. Although their prewar business would be reduced, if not ruined, the Ysabels were probably better fixed than Belle in the matter of earning a living. They were Texas frontiersmen, with the great wide spread of the Lone Star State in which to search for a fresh start.

Big, powerfully built, Sam Ysabel had short-cropped black hair and a rugged face tanned to the color of old saddle leather, but was clean-shaven in honor of the occasion. He wore a fringed buckskin shirt and trousers, with Comanche moccasins on his feet. A battered old Confederate Jeff Davis campaign hat dangled from the back of his chair. Around his waist hung a gun belt, supporting an old Dragoon Colt, its butt pointing forward, at the left side, and on the right a sheathed bowie knife.

Almost as tall as his father, Loncey Dalton Ysabel had a slim, wiry frame that hinted at hidden reserves of strength. Hair as black as the wing of a Deep South crow framed a handsome, Indian-dark face with a young, almost babishly innocent cast of features. His red-hazel eyes seemed out of place in such a face, being neither young nor innocent, but giving a hint of his true, reckless nature. He wore all black clothing, including the wide-brimmed, low-crowned Stetson hat hanging on his chair and the gun belt about his lean waist. Reversing his father's style of armament, he carried his walnut-handled Dragoon Colt in a low cavalry twist-draw holster on his right thigh and an ivory-hilted James Black bowie knife sheathed at his left hip. There were few people along the Rio Grande's banks who would have regarded those weapons as being mere decorations.

Born in the village of the *Pehnane*—Wasp, Quick Stinger, Raider—Comanche, the tall, slim, young Texan had been brought up and educated as a member of that hardy warrior race. Sam Ysabel's wife, daughter of Chief Long Walker and his French Creole *pairaivo*,* had died giving birth to their only child. With his father away much of the time on the family business of first mustanging, then smuggling, the boy had been raised by his maternal grandfather. War leader of the Dog Soldier lodge, Long Walker had taught his grandson all those things a *Pehnane* brave heart must know.† The boy had grown up skilled in the use of both white and red man's weapons, capable of winning the confidence or mastering any horse ever foaled, able to follow barely discernible tracks and to locate hidden enemies or to conceal himself from the most keen-eyed searchers.

Following his father along the Rio Grande's smuggling trails, the boy had put his *Pehnane* education to good use. He had also earned himself considerable fame in the bloody border country. By virtue of his exceptional skill when wielding one, the *Pehnane* had given him the man-name *"Cuchillo,"* the

* *Pairaivo:* favorite wife.
† Told in *Comanche*.

Knife. To the Mexicans with whom he came in contact, he was *"Cabrito,"* the Kid. Among the Texans, he was known as "the Ysabel Kid". Members of all three races, fighting men from soda to hock, recognized his fatal accuracy when shooting a Mississippi rifle and acknowledged that he could perform adequately with his old Dragoon or knife. All were unanimous in their belief that he made a real good, loyal friend, but was a deadly, implacable foe.

On learning of the War Between the States, the Ysabels had traveled East and enlisted in John Singleton Mosby's Raiders. Although the Gray Ghost had thought highly of their ability as scouts, he had been compelled to let them return to Texas. There they had continued to render important service to the South by delivering urgently needed supplies—run through the U.S. Navy's blockade into neutral Matamoros—across the Rio Grande to the Confederate authorities.

It had been during this work that they had met the Rebel Spy. Sent to negotiate with a French general, who had offered to throw his full command into the war on the side of the Confederate States, Belle had been assigned the Ysabels as her escort. Fortunately for her, circumstances had prevented Belle from completing the mission.* Generals Grant and Lee had met at the Appomattox Courthouse, as the first move toward ending the war, on the day that she should have contacted the French renegade and handed over the advance payment for his services.

That had been just over six months ago. On their return to Matamoros, news of the war's end had not yet arrived. So the Confederate States consul had asked them to leave as quickly as possible. The ambiguous diplomatic situation in the town had caused him to make the request. Neither of the warring governments north of the border wished to antagonize the Mexican patriots or the European powers involved in the struggle for control of Mexico. Knowing that Belle's mission might be ex-

* Told in *The Bloody Border*.

ploited by the Yankees as a means of discrediting his consulate, the consul had taken steps to remove her and her assistants.

Being aware of the consul's motives, Belle had taken a ship to Nassau, the principal port for blockade runners in the West Indies. It had been her intention to go on to Charleston, or Savannah, from either of which Confederate towns she could report to her superiors for further orders. On hearing that the war had ended, she returned to Matamoros with the intention of spreading the news in Texas and ending the fighting between the Rebels and the Yankees defending Brownsville.

On arrival in Matamoros, she had learned that the news was known. The consulate no longer had any official status, but its consul had remained in Mexico as a private citizen. Wanting to learn all she could about conditions north of the Rio Grande, Belle had crossed over and in Brownsville had met the Ysabels. From what they had told her, they had spent their enforced absence with the *Pehnane* Comanche. The Kid had been hoping to locate a boyhood enemy, No Father, and settle accounts with him, but failed to do so.* Coming back to Matamoros, the Ysabels had found that their services were no longer required officially and were making their first visit to Brownsville since the start of the Yankee occupation.

Accepting the Ysabels' offer to have a meal with them, Belle had been surprised when they brought her to Bannister's Hotel. One of the town's best-known establishments, it now appeared to cater to businessmen who had carved a niche during the Union's control. However, its owner raised no objections to the Ysabel family entering with their guest. The food had been good and the disapproving glares thrown their way by the room's other occupants failed to spoil Belle's appetite. Not until they had finished the meal did the subject of the future come up.

"What will you do now, Sam?" Belle asked, sitting opposite the big man and with the Kid on her left.

"Ain't made our minds up yet," Ysabel admitted.

* How the Kid settled his account with No Father is told in *Sidewinder*.

"Could start selling maps to where we buried all that money we was taking to the Frog general, *ap',* " suggested the Kid with a grin, using the Comanche word for father.

"But we destroyed the money," Belle objected.

"You know it, we know it," the Kid answered. "Trouble being, nobody believes us that that's what happened."

"We've had three different fellers asking us about it," Ysabel confirmed.

Belle smiled, knowing that the money in question was irrecoverable at the bottom of the Rio Grande.

"I can't see you as treasure-map sellers," she told the Texans.

"Anyways, we'll make out fine one way or another," Ysabel assured her. "Right now it's you we're thinking about."

"Why don't you stay on here in Brownsville and help us set up again, Miss Belle?" asked the Kid. "It's not going to be easy for roughnecks like us to do it, is it, *ap'?*"

"Sure ain't, boy," Ysabel confirmed. "Most all the folks we used to trade with don't have money no more to buy smuggled wine and stuff."

That Belle could figure out without needing to ask for an explanation. By its support of the Confederate States, Texas had been left with a worthless currency. The majority of the Ysabels' old customers would be broke, or near to it. For some time to come they would be too busy striving for survival and the recovery of their state's solvency to be able to afford smuggled luxuries.* Yet there were others, people whose loyalties had been with the victorious North, who might possess the means to purchase the Ysabels' wares. As Sam Ysabel had said, contacting such new customers would not be easy.

There was one big snag to Belle accepting the offer and helping the Ysabel family to gather sufficient customers to make their business pay. Even before the assassination of President Lincoln, the liberals, radicals and intellectuals of the Union had been demanding that extreme reprisals be carried out against

* The way in which Texas recovered is told in *Goodnight's Dream* and *From Hide and Horn.*

the supporters of the Confederacy. With the blind, bigoted in-
tolerance their kind always showed against anybody who dared
to oppose their lofty ideals, the Northern soft-shells had repeatedly demanded that every Southern leader be hanged for trea-
son. Having caused some of the soft-shells inconvenience,
humiliation and loss, Belle had heard that she and Rose Greenhow were to receive the same treatment if captured. So she had
no desire to fall into the Yankees' hands until she had discovered how much power and authority the soft-shells would command in the United States government.

Wondering how she could frame a refusal that would not
offend the Texans, Belle heard a disturbance from the hotel's
lobby. Raucous laughter and loud talk rose, drawing the attention of all the diners to the door of the room. Turning her head
to the right, Belle saw a quartet of sailors had entered the
building. Judging by their general appearance of conviviality
and the increase to their nautical rolling gait, the newcomers
had been drinking steadily and long. Clad in the usual dark
blue, round, peakless cap, blouse and bell-bottomed trousers of
the United States Navy, each of them had a cutlass dangling
from the left side of his belt and a Colt Navy revolver in a high-
riding, close-topped holster at its right.

Before the war, ordinary seamen would not have been encouraged to remain in Bannister's Hotel, and the quartet
clearly knew it. Conscious of their status as victors in a con-
quered city, they showed disdain for the management's preju-
dices. Halting just outside the dining room's door, they looked
around until their eyes came to rest on Belle, the youngest and
best-looking woman present.

Although the Ysabels hardly gave the sailors more than a
glance, Belle treated them to a longer scrutiny. All were tall:
one a big, thickset, clean-shaven stoker, two leaner, dark-
headed and bearded—and the last a gangling beanpole with
sandy red hair.

Early in her career as a spy, Belle had found that she possessed a talent of the greatest use and did her best to develop it.
She had a remarkable memory for faces and, more important,

the ability to recall the circumstances which led her to remember them. Stiffening slightly, she halted her right hand as it moved involuntarily toward the parasol leaning against her chair.

"What's up, Miss Belle?" demanded the Kid, having noticed the girl's gesture.

"I've seen that ginger-haired sailor before," Belle replied, turning her attention hurriedly toward her companions as the sailors' gaze moved her way. "He was one of the pair who tried to pull me into the guard boat the night we attacked the *Waterbury*."

"Reckon he'll recognize you?" asked Ysabel, suddenly realizing that it might go badly for the girl should she be identified as the Rebel Spy.

"I hope not," Belle answered. "Damn it, they're coming over here."

Having completed their examination of the room and satisfied themselves that only civilians were present, the sailors swaggered forward. If the man with ginger hair recognized Belle as the girl who had been captured, but escaped, on the night that the U.S. Navy's steam sloop *Waterbury* had been torpedoed in Brownsville harbor, he showed no sign of it. Instead he seemed to be jockeying for position with his companions. Coming to a halt at the empty side of the table, the quartet eyed Sam Ysabel and the Kid in the challenging manner before turning their lecherous gaze in Belle's direction.

"These land crabs don't look to be giving you much of a time, gal," the stoker exclaimed in a loud voice.

"Why, they're my uncle and cousin from out of town, sir," Belle answered, giving the Kid's leg a quick kick as he seemed about to speak. "We've just finished supper and are going home."

"They don't look like your kin," declared one of the black-haired pair and looked at the other. "Do they, Mick?"

"Not all that much, Joe," Mick replied.

"She's a niece on my wife's side," Ysabel rumbled.

"Was you pair in the Reb army?" demanded Joe belligerently.

"The war's over, sailor," Belle put in, studiously avoiding looking at the ginger-haired man.

"And we won it," the stoker pointed out. "Anyways, it's too early for a pretty gal like you to be going home."

"It sure is, Cully." Mick grinned. "And she shouldn't be going home with no kinfolks neither."

Swiftly Belle looked around the room. Its other occupants showed signs of resentment or concern. They were middle-aged couples, reasonably prosperous-looking and not the kind to become involved in anything as unseemly as the behavior of the sailors. Knowing there would be no help from that source, Belle hoped to be able to avert trouble.

At which point Belle became aware of the ginger man's eyes on her. Moving around his companions, he halted close to the girl and was studying her with extra interest. To add to Belle's discomfort, she recollected that she had not troubled to don a wig, or any other form of disguise, before crossing from Matamoros. So, apart from being dry, she looked much the same as she had when the sailor had last seen her.

"That's truly true, Mick," the stoker said. "And being so, we can't let you do it, gal."

"Who'd you reckon she should go home with, *hombre*?" asked the Kid in a mild, gentle tone that would have shrieked warnings to anybody who knew him.

"Us, beefhead. Us!" Cully answered. "So you can push off and leave us see her safe to port."

"Why I do declare I'm honored, gentlemen," Belle gushed before either of the Ysabels could speak. "But there'd be four of you-all and only the one of lil me. I just couldn't be attentive to more than one of you-all. It wouldn't be proper."

Apparently that point had not struck the four sailors. Finding the girl willing to accept the company of one of them came as a surprise and raised difficulties. Some of the quartet's hostility was diverted from the Ysabels and to each other as they wondered who should take precedence with the girl. Nor did

Belle help matters. Glancing from face to face, she seemed to exude a welcome and promise to each of the sailors and made the recipient feel that he was the one she favored.

Catching his father's eye, the Kid sank into a casual-seeming slouch on the chair. Both of them knew that the sailors were looking for trouble, so they prepared to deal with it. A quick inclination of Ysabel's head told the Kid how he aimed to make his play should the need arise. Slowly, so as to arouse no suspicion, Ysabel placed the palms of his hands under the edge of the table. Drawing no more attention to himself, the Kid duplicated his father's move. Then they waited, tense as coil springs under pressure, watching for the first hostile word or gesture from the other four.

For her part, Belle also studied the sailors. She hoped that she had prevented a clash between them and the Ysabels. During her assignments with them, she had seen her companions in action and knew that they had small regard for the sanctity of human life. While she did not doubt the two Texans' ability to protect themselves, she knew that doing so might lead them into very serious trouble. Just let one of the sailors be killed, no matter how much provocation had been heaped on the Ysabels, and a military court would show them no mercy. With that in mind, Belle went on with her attempt at setting the quartet at each other's throats.

"If you gentlemen just tell me which of you I'll have the honor to be escorted home by," Belle went on, uncomfortably aware of the ginger-haired sailor's scrutiny, "I'm right sure my kinsfolk won't—"

"Hey!" yelped the ginger man, stabbing a finger in Belle's direction. "I've seen you afore."

"Don't try that one, Carrots!" Cully, the stoker, growled. "The gal's going with me."

"She never said so," protested Mick indignantly. "I reckon she—"

Stabbing forward his left hand, Carrots placed it on Belle's right shoulder and started to turn her toward him. Before his companions, or the Ysabels, could object, he leaned forward to stare directly into the girl's face.

"It's her, damn it!" Carrots screeched. "She's the Rebel Spy. I saw her—"

2
IF YOU'VE MADE ME
LOSE THEM

As soon as Carrots laid hands on her, Belle reached for the parasol with her right hand and her left slipped her reticule's strings free from the back of her chair. Hearing his words, she started to rise. While doing so, she propelled the parasol upward sharply. Driving toward the sailor's chin, the silver knob at the end of the handle rammed with considerable force against his prominent Adam's apple. Just too late to prevent him from making his denunciation, the pain of the impact chopped off the rest of Carrots' words. With hands rising to clutch at the stricken area, he released the girl's shoulder and stumbled back a few paces. Freed from Carrots' restraint, Belle continued to stand up.

Seeing Belle launch her attack, the Ysabel family went into action. Shoving back with his knees, the Kid sent his chair skidding away from beneath him. Then he lunged erect and heaved at his edge of the table. Timing his moves to coincide with his son's, Sam Ysabel also rose. Lifting the table between them, they hurled it at the remaining three sailors.

Turning edgeways to the floor and spraying the utensils and crockery it had supported from its top, the table struck Cully and Joe, hurling them back. Although he was no less surprised by the sudden turn of events, Mick managed to throw himself toward the wall and avoided being hit by the Ysabels' missile. Doing so proved to be a mistake. In fact he might have wished that he had stood his ground and taken his punishment like a man.

Noticing that Mick had not been driven to the rear with his companions, Ysabel swung in his direction. Up lashed the big Texan's left leg. Years of wearing no other covering than moccasins had hardened Ysabel's feet to a considerable degree and made them effective weapons. Caught in the groin by the kick, Mick let out a screech of pain, folded over and collapsed. Almost before his victim had landed, Ysabel was snatching his hat from the chair's back and ramming it onto his head.

"Get out of here!" Belle yelled, turning to do so.

While in full agreement with the girl's suggestion, Sam Ysabel and the Kid knew that carrying it out would not be an easy matter. The table might have forced Cully and Joe to withdraw for long enough to give Ysabel time to render Mick *hors de combat,* but it had in no way incapacitated the other two sailors. They and Carrots were still capable of disputing the three Southerners' departure.

Pitching the table out of the way, Cully bellowed in fury and hurled himself at Ysabel. Stoking the boilers of a coal-burning warship was not a task to be performed by weaklings and Cully was noted in the U.S. Navy for his strength. He used it in a fight to smash down all resistance by sheer force. Looking as huge and dangerous as a charging buffalo bull, he rushed toward the Texan with hamlike hands reaching out to seize and crush.

Being a more cautious man than Cully, even when drunk, Joe was content to let the stoker avenge the attack on his brother. The Kid had sprung into the center of the room after throwing over the table and looked a safer subject for reprisals than his father. Clenching his fists, Joe went toward the Indian-dark youngster. While approaching, the sailor saw a change come over his intended victim. Up to that moment, the Kid had looked like a very young and harmless boy. Suddenly all the babyish innocence left his face, being replaced by the cold, savage, slit-eyed expression of a *Pehnane* Dog Soldier waiting to take on an enemy. Flashing across, the Kid's right hand closed about the hilt of the bowie knife and started to slide the eleven-and-a-half-inch-long, two-and-a-half-inch-wide, clip-pointed blade from its sheath.

Few people who knew the Ysabel Kid would have given Joe a life expectancy exceeding the time he took to come within striking distance of the other's black-sleeved right arm.

Seeing Belle darting in his direction and transferring the reticule into her parasol-filled right hand, Carrots tore his thoughts from his half-strangled condition. As the girl swerved to go by him, he shot out his hands to catch her by the right wrist and bicep. Having received one taste of the parasol's handle, he had no wish to repeat the dose. With the girl's right arm immobilized, he felt sure that she was helpless. Bringing her to a halt at arm's length in front of him, he started to imagine the commendation and promotion that would come his way as a reward for capturing the Rebel Spy.

For all his bulk, Sam Ysabel could move with surprising speed. Springing forward as if meaning to meet Cully head-on, Ysabel swerved aside at the last moment. Powerful hands clamped hold of Cully's left wrist. Taking a firm grip, Ysabel heaved the stoker onward. Narrowly missing a collision with Joe, Cully felt himself hauled around in a half circle. Combined with the stoker's own momentum, Ysabel's pull built up an uncontrollable speed. Then Ysabel released his hold. On being turned loose, Cully could not prevent himself plunging across the room. A waiter flung himself hurriedly from the stoker's path. Ahead was a window, but Cully could neither stop himself nor swerve aside. Barely managing to do more than throw up his hands to protect his face, Cully went through the window. Crashing to the sidewalk, he rolled across it to drop onto the street.

Hearing the shattering crash of breaking glass, an infantry patrol farther along the street halted and did a rapid about-face to see what caused it. Being assigned to the duty of policing the town, the lieutenant in command knew that he must investigate. He had seen the four sailors before they had entered the hotel and marked them as potential trouble-causers. Having also noted the size and brawn of Cully in particular, he wanted his men as fresh as possible while dealing with the quartet. So he led them back over the hundred or so yards separating them from the building at a quick march instead of on the double.

Despite having her right arm held, Belle was far from helpless. Balancing on her right leg, she shot her left foot behind her. The heel of her boot spiked onto Carrots' kneecap, driven by a powerful set of leg muscles. Pain ripped through the lean man. Letting go of the girl's arm, he hopped back and tried to support his injured knee with his hands. Unfortunately for him, he did not retreat sufficiently far before doing so. Spinning around, Belle used her turning momentum to add force to her knotted left fist. It swung not in the manner of a frightened girl, but with trained purpose. Hard knuckles met Carrots' jaw with a sharp click. Off balance, he spun around and went headfirst into the wall. Bouncing back, he flopped as limp as a rag doll to the floor.

With his knife half drawn, the Kid recalled his father's orders. Few people in Texas had ever regarded smuggling, as carried out by the Ysabel family, as a serious crime. Even the U.S. military authorities had tended to ignore it before the war and, provided they received their share of the goods, would most likely continue to do so. However, Ysabel knew that no such tolerance could be expected if a Yankee serviceman should be killed. So he had repeatedly warned his son that weapons must only be used as a last resort if they were forced to lock horns with their erstwhile enemies.

Restraining his first impulse to produce and make use of the bowie knife, the Kid returned it to the sheath and took his hand from the hilt. Already Joe was closing in and his right fist lashed savagely at the young Texan's head.

Deprived of his favorite close-quarters weapon, the Kid was still far from being easy meat. While the Comanches preferred more direct, permanent ways of dealing with an enemy, they had not been unmindful of the possibility that an attack might come at a time when no weapon was available. So they had developed various barehanded fighting tricks to meet such situations. The Kid had received a thorough training in *Nemenuh*** wrestling techniques.

Throwing up his left hand inside Joe's advancing right arm, the Kid deftly prevented the punch from reaching his head and caught the other's wrist. At the same time, the Kid started to pivot to his left. His right arm rose, working in concert with the other movements, passing beneath Joe's right armpit and behind the sailor's bicep. Continuing to turn and sinking into a kneeling position on his bent right leg, the Kid heaved on the trapped arm. Feeling his feet leave the floor and body rise into the air, Joe let out a startled wail. Released as he passed above the Kid's shoulder, Joe smashed down hard on his back.

After liberating herself and felling Carrots, Belle swung ready to lend her companions assistance. She gripped the parasol in both hands. Designed for her work, its innocent exterior concealed a powerful steel-spring billy of considerable strength and effectiveness. Seeing that her help would not be needed, she left the parasol intact.

"Come on!" she yelled, turning in the direction of the door.

Although the other guests were on their feet, none tried to interfere with the trio as they ran from the room. The Kid had retrieved his hat before leaving and donned it as he followed his father and Belle from the hotel.

"Hey you!" yelled the patrol commander. "Halt right there!"

"Like hell!" Ysabel growled, glancing at the unconscious stoker. "Cross over and go down between Orley's saloon and that undertaker's parlor, Miss Belle. We'll lose 'em easy enough in the back streets."

Obediently, the girl bounded from the sidewalk and sped diagonally across the street in the direction indicated by the big Texan. Wanting to shield her if the patrol started shooting, the

* *Nemenuh:* the People, the Comanches' name for their tribe.

Ysabels allowed the girl to draw ahead. Belle set a fast pace, taking a line that would keep them out of the lighted area before the saloon. While he shouted another command to halt, the Yankee officer did not order his men to open fire. Instead, they gave chase, running as fast as they could in their overcoats, accoutrements and heavy Jefferson bootees and armed with Springfield muzzle-loading rifles.

Approaching the front of the saloon, Belle saw three men walk out. Hearing the sounds of the chase, the trio turned to investigate. A gasp burst from Belle and she skidded to a halt, staring at the men as if she could not believe the evidence of her eyes.

"Tollinger!" she gasped.

Following the direction of Belle's gaze, the Ysabels wondered at her reaction. They had noticed the three men, but attached no importance to them as none wore uniforms or showed other signs of official capacity.

Dressed in town suits, with vests, white shirts and red neckties, two of the men's appearance gave no clue as to who or what they might be. Sporting a derby hat, the taller of them was gaunt, with a sallow face that a thick-lipped, petulant mouth, hollow cheeks and sunken eyes gave a mean, arrogant expression. Bareheaded, the other had a portly build. His surly, piggish cast of features were not improved by a drooping black moustache and lank, greasy long hair.

The third man hardly seemed likely company for the other two. Middle-sized, stocky, he was a Mexican with an evil face that carried a scar running down its left cheek and along his neck until hidden by the *serape* draped over his shoulders. A gray *sombrero* perched on the back of his head and the *serape* covered him to the knees, effectively concealing any weapons he might be carrying.

Even as the word left the girl's lips, the Kid collided with her. Staggering, she might have fallen but for Sam Ysabel. Leaping forward, he scooped Belle up under his right arm. Without breaking his stride, he continued to run toward the alley.

Glancing at the three men in passing, the Kid recognized the Mexican and saw shock twist at the faces of the two white men. Snarling something that did not reach the Kid's ears, the taller of the pair made as if to move forward. Catching his arm, the other dude spoke quietly but urgently in his ear. Then the Kid raced by, following his father.

"Let me down!" Belle gasped, kicking her legs and struggling in Ysabel's grasp. "If you made me lose them, I'll—"

Dropping the girl to her feet as they rounded the corner of the building, Ysabel expected her to follow him. Instead she made as if to return to the street. Grabbing her by the wrist, he jerked her after him. Sanity returned to Belle as she was on the point of resisting and she yielded to his pull.

" 'Round the corner there!" Ysabel ordered, indicating the rear end of the undertaker's parlor. "Reckon you can lead 'em off, boy?"

"Nothing easier," drawled the Kid, drawing and cocking his old Dragoon.

Lengthening his stride, the youngster drew ahead. His black clothing soon rendered him invisible in the darkness. Looking back over her shoulder, Belle half expected to see the men from the saloon following her. Nobody had appeared so far. Changing his hold from the wrist to her bicep, Ysabel guided her around the corner. With the clumping of heavy boots drawing closer, they came to an involuntary halt.

"Hell's fires!" Ysabel spat out. "He's built a wall since we was last here."

Rising a good eight feet high, the plank wall extended from the rear of the undertaker's premises for a disconcertingly indefinite distance, merging into the darkness without giving any sign of coming to an end. For some reason, it had been erected from a point about a yard along the building instead of at the corner. So they had failed to notice it until too late.

Already the patrol had reached the mouth of the alley. Climbing the obstruction could not be accomplished silently enough to escape detection; nor could Belle and Ysabel retreat and follow the Kid.

Even as the girl and the Texan became aware of their predicament, they heard the sound of a shot. Not the high-pitched crack a Springfield would make, but the deep boom caused by igniting forty grains of powder in the uppermost chamber of a Dragoon Colt's cylinder. It rang out from the direction taken by the Kid.

"What—!" Belle began, starting to turn as startled exclamations rose and the patrol's boot thuds came to a stop.

Instantly Ysabel's hands gripped her shoulders, forcing her to face the wall. Another shot boomed from the Dragoon and Ysabel kept Belle motionless while drawing his own revolver.

"There they are!" bawled a voice from the mouth of the valley.

"Stay put!" Ysabel hissed in Belle's ear as two rifles cracked. "It's Lon's way of making sure they follow him."

"Stop that shooting, damn you!" barked the officer. "Come on!"

"Real still now, Miss Belle!" whispered Ysabel. "Don't turn and we're safe."

Suddenly Belle understood her companion's insistence that she remain motionless. If she had turned, the white of her blouse might have caught the attention of the passing soldiers. Hardly daring to breathe, she stood as if turned to stone and followed the progress of their pursuers with her ears. They continued by the end of the building. Waiting to catch any comment that would mean the Yankees' bullets had hit the Kid, Belle gave an involuntary jump as one of them shouted:

"There they go!"

"Get after them!" roared the officer.

When the sounds of the pursuit had faded away, Ysabel allowed Belle to turn from the fence.

"Sorry I had to rough-handle you that ways, Miss Belle," he said and holstered his Colt. "Only I didn't want you turning—"

"I know why," Belle interrupted. "Lon's still all right."

"Trust him for that." Ysabel grinned. "Say, what was up on the street? Do you know *Cicatriz*?"

"*Cica*—You mean the Mexican?"

"Yes'm."

"I've never seen him. It was the other two. They're the men who murdered my parents."

"The hell you say!" Ysabel growled.

For a moment Belle did not speak. A shudder ran through her slender frame and she shook her head from side to side, as if trying to blot out the memory. Ysabel waited in silence. With an effort, the girl regained control of her feelings.

"Thanks for your help, Sam," she said. "I'll be going now."

"After them?" Ysabel inquired.

"Yes!"

"Leave it a minute, then we'll both go," suggested Ysabel.

"It's not your quarrel, Sam," Belle pointed out.

"Maybe not," the big Texan grunted. "But with *Cicatriz* sitting in the game, you'll need help. So I'm coming, 'less you say I shouldn't."

"Tollinger and Barmain may still work for the Yankee Secret Service," Belle warned, "And I mean to kill them both."

"Which I don't blame you for," Ysabel replied. "So, if you want it, you've got Lon 'n' me siding you."

Belle did not reply immediately. During the mission they had shared, she had come to know the Ysabel family very well and formed the highest opinion of their sterling qualities. There could be only one answer to the magnanimous offer.

"Thank you, Sam," she said. "I'd admire to have you with me."

While waiting for Ysabel's minute, Belle learned that *Cicatriz*, the Scar, was a notorious border *bandido*. They briefly debated the reason for the Mexican being with her enemies, but reached no conclusions. No further shooting sounded, which implied that the patrol had not caught up with the Kid. At last Ysabel led the way to the street, but they saw no sign of the three men. Ysabel asked Belle to remain in hiding while he conducted inquiries in the saloon. On Belle agreeing, he went to the rear of that building and returned within five minutes.

"Seems like they was only waiting there for *Cicatriz*," the big

Texan remarked as he and Belle walked off through the darkness. "Orley don't know anything about 'em; and he's a good enough friend to tell me if he did. Do you reckon they knowed it was you?"

"That's what's been puzzling me, Sam," Belle replied, "I'm almost sure that they recognized me, especially as I said Tollinger's name. So I wonder why they didn't tell the patrol who I am, or come with them to help hunt me down."

"Do they know you're after them?"

"I've never made any great secret of it."

"We don't know they recognized you," Ysabel pointed out. "They for sure didn't tell the puddle-splashers. Them soldiers didn't stop until Lon throwed lead their way."

Leading Belle through the darkened streets into the poorer white residential section, Ysabel insisted that they should behave in a natural manner. The Kid joined them as they approached a house standing in the center of a garden surrounded by a picket fence.

"Lon!" Belle greeted. "You're safe!"

"Why wouldn't I be?" asked the Kid. "Shucks, I near on had to whistle, whoop 'n' wave a couple of times to stop them blue bellies losing me."

Pressed by Belle for further details, the Kid explained briefly how he had drawn the patrol to the fringes of the Mexican section before giving them the slip. Although no rendezvous had been arranged, he guessed that his father would bring the girl to Ma O'Grady's rooming house—the family's headquarters in Brownsville—and so had made his way there. Learning of the reason for Belle's behavior outside the saloon, the Kid disagreed with the summation that she and his father had made.

"Way them two acted, I'd say they knowed you, Miss Belle," the youngster stated. "The tall jasper made like he was fixing to come after you, but his *amigo* stopped him."

"Then *I* don't know what to make of it." Belle sighed. "They know I've sworn to kill them."

"Could be they don't want the Army to know they're

around," the Kid offered. "Or figure to get you killed without the blue bellies knowing about it, seeing's the Army's playing fair with folks here in Brownsville and don't want trouble."

"Either's possible," Belle admitted.

"If it's the last," Ysabel said soberly, "they've got real good help on hand to get you killed."

"The Mexican?" Belle guessed.

"Cicatriz," confirmed Ysabel. "You being a woman wouldn't make no never mind to him."

"If the price was right," drawled the Kid, "he'd kill you, or fix it done, Miss Belle. Would them two *hombres* know you're back in town?"

"It's not likely," Belle said after a moment's thought.

"Anyways," said the Kid, with the air of one who had solved a difficult problem, and opened the picket fence's gate. "I don't see what all the talking's about. There's one feller's can likely give us all the answers."

"Who?" asked Belle.

"Cicatriz," replied the Kid.

3

BAD DON'T EVEN START TO COVER IT

Halting just inside the gate, Belle looked from the Kid to his father and back again.

"Do you know where to find him?" she asked.

"We know where to go ask about him, for starters," Ysabel replied. "He mostly hangs out around Cisco Castro's *cantina.*"

"Let's go and see if he's there," Belle said eagerly. "They might be with him."

"Not if they've got the sense of a seam squirrel between 'em," the Kid growled. "You can die through just breathing the air in Castro's *cantina,* you don't even need to drink his liquor."

"Comes to a point," Ysabel continued, "I wouldn't like to say who's the most ornery, him or *Cicatriz.* Anyways, you can't come with us, Miss Belle. Castro's is no place for a lady."

"I've been told that a lady wouldn't become a spy." Belle smiled. "So I'm coming with you. I've been in some pretty bad places, you know."

"Not's bad's Castro's place," Ysabel contradicted.

"That's for sure," the Kid agreed. "Bad don't even start to cover it."

"I'm still coming with you!" Belle stated, setting her face grimly. "No arguments, boys. I've made up my mind on that score."

The Kid gave an overdone sigh of resignation, but his lips curled in an admiring grin as he looked at the girl. If ever he had seen determination personified, it was Belle at that moment.

"Do you have any of them fancy disguises with you, ma'am?" Ysabel inquired, also yielding to the inevitable.

"Only what I'm wearing," Belle replied. "My wigs are with my other gear at our consulate in Matamoros. I think I can fix something up, if I've anywhere to do it."

"I hope finding *Cicatriz*'s as easy," Ysabel told her and led the way along the path.

Before they reached the house, its front door opened. A big buxom, white-haired woman stepped onto the porch. Neatly dressed, she held a Navy Colt in her right hand with casual competence.

"Oh, 'tis you, Big Sam," the woman greeted, letting the revolver's barrel sag out of line. "When I heard three of yez coming, I didn't know who it might be."

"This here's Miss Boyd, Ma," Ysabel introduced, joining the woman on the porch. "Can you put her up for the night?"

Before answering, Ma O'Grady looked Belle over from head to foot. The old woman read quality and breeding in the girl's face and bearing. That was no tail-peddler from a whorehouse; not that the Ysabels would bring such a person to Ma's home.

"It's not grand, like you've been used to," Ma told Belle at last. "But it's clean and you're welcome to stay."

"Thank you," Belle answered, smiling. "That's very good of you, especially taken with the company I'm keeping."

"I thought you was trying to improve 'em maybe." Ma grinned. "There's room for plenty of that. Come on in, all of you."

With that, Ma ushered Belle and the Texans into the house and closed the door. Taking them into the small, clean and comfortably furnished sitting room, she offered the girl the best chair and asked if Belle would care for a meal.

"We already ate, Ma," Ysabel put in. "Got to go out again for a spell after Miss Belle's changed clothes."

"Out?" Ma snorted. "And where'd you be taking a young lady to at this hour, Big Sam?"

"Cisco Castro's *cantina,*" the Kid answered when his father hesitated.

"Don't you go making fun of a poor, defenseless old body like me, Lon Ysabel!" Ma warned, swinging belligerently toward the youngster. "Sure and he's lost all his respect while he's been away, Big Sam."

"He sure has, Ma," agreed Ysabel. "Only he told you the truth."

Giving the woman no chance to protest, Ysabel explained why he and the Kid would be taking Belle to Castro's *cantina.* Listening in silence, Ma kept her eyes on the girl whose name had become a legend during the war years. For her part, Belle stiffened slightly and waited to see Ma show condemnation on learning that she intended to avenge her parents' murders. None came. Instead, Ma nodded approval. When Ysabel stopped talking, the old woman showed that she had not only followed his explanation but also formed conclusions.

"You can't go dressed like that," Ma declared, indicating Belle's clothes. "Maybe I can help. Had a gal rooming here in the last weeks of the war. She'd been working in a saloon, but married a sailor. They went off home a month back, but she left some of her work clothes behind. If they're any use to you—"

"Can I take a look at them?" Belle asked.

"Come up to your room and I'll fetch 'em along to you," Ma replied.

Collecting and lighting a lamp, Ma escorted Belle upstairs and into a small bedroom at the rear of the building. Like the rest of the house, its furnishings were not new. However, the bed looked comfortable and had clean sheets and pillowcases. Crossing to the window, Ma drew its curtains together. Then she turned and looked at the girl.

"Will it do?"

"It's the best room I've had for some time," Belle replied, placing her parasol and reticule on the bed.

"I'll go and fetch up Dolly's gear then," Ma decided. "It may take me a while to find it."

"That's all right, Ma," Belle assured her. "I've a few things to do."

After Ma had left the room, Belle hung her coat in the wardrobe and returned to the bed. Tugging at the side of her waistband, she set free her skirt and it fell to the floor around her feet. Encased in black silk stockings, her legs had a dancer's shapely, well-developed muscles. Removing her blouse left her clad in brief underclothing of a style not usually worn by well-bred Southern ladies.

Gathering up the skirt, Belle turned it inside out. Like the parasol, the skirt had been made with the needs of her profession in mind. Although the outer side had been plain, inside was a lining of glossy material. From the skirt, Belle turned her attention to the blouse. Taking a small pair of scissors from her reticule, she set to work removing the decorous frilly ruffle from its bosom.

On her return, carrying a leather case and a hatbox, Ma slammed to a halt and stared at the transformed Belle. The blouse, turned inside out, was of a shiny white material, sleeveless and with a daring décolleté. Drawn tighter, the skirt emphasized the rich curves of her hips but looked cheap and flashy.

"The saints preserve us!" Ma ejaculated. "How'd you do that?"

"These clothes were especially made for me," Belle replied, going across and relieving the woman of the case.

Examining the belongings of the departed ex-saloon girl, Belle found all she would need to make her disguise acceptable. Despite the alterations to her clothes, she had known there were other touches required to make her look the part. So she helped herself to a hat that would conceal the shortness of her hair, some cheap jewelry and a fancy shawl. Swiftly she applied some of Dolly's discarded makeup to her face.

"How do I look?" Belle asked, entering the sitting room and turning around before the Kid and his father.

"Just like the sort of gal who'd go into Castro's place," Ysabel praised.

"We'd better go out the back way," Belle suggested as the men prepared to leave. "I don't want to spoil Ma's good name in the neighborhood."

"Don't let that worry you, Miss Belle," Ma answered. "I can outcuss anybody on this street, and I know enough about them all to make them keep quiet."

Despite Ma's assurances, Belle and the Ysabels elected to leave by the back door. Doing so gave Belle her first view of the rear side of the property. Going by all appearances, the old woman ran a livery barn in addition to the rooming house. As she went by the open doors of the big barn, Belle saw her companions' horses in the stalls. Knowing the two Texans' dislike for walking, she expected them to go and collect the animals.

"We'll walk over there," Ysabel said, interpreting her look correctly. "It'll be easier'n riding, if we have to leave in a hurry."

At first Belle could not follow the reasoning behind Ysabel's statement, but understanding soon came. They passed through an increasingly poorer white section of the town, until it merged with the Mexican quarter. The change showed chiefly in the selection of building materials, although the smells which came to Belle's nose grew subtly different. Instead of wooden shacks, the buildings were adobe *jacales,* gradually getting smaller in size and closer together. She could see that riding a horse at speed through the narrow, winding streets would be hazardous in the extreme and how escaping on foot might offer a better chance of safety.

Watching the way in which her companions kept their hands hovering near their weapons, Belle gripped her reticule tightly in her left hand and the right tightened on the handle of the parasol. Closing protectively on either side of the girl, the Ysabels stayed alert for any warning sound or movement. Belle did not blame them for the precautions. Cold eyes watched them from all sides and occasionally a silent shape would flicker across their path then disappear into the shadows.

"There it is," Ysabel announced, pointing ahead.

They stood on the edge of a small plaza. At the other side, dwarfing the surrounding buildings with its two-story height and considerable length, Castro's *cantina* glowed with lights, music and rowdy merriment. As the trio crossed the plaza, a pair of bulky Mexicans hauled a smaller member of their race outside and hurled him headlong into the gutter. Dragging himself up, moaning and clasping at a bloody gash on his cheek, the evicted man stumbled away. For a moment the two bouncers stared at the girl and the Ysabels, then turned and walked back inside.

"Maybe he spit on the floor," drawled the Kid in answer to Belle's unspoken question. "Ole Cisco's real touchy about folks doing things like that. Other things, he's not so touchy about."

"Stick close, Miss Belle," Ysabel ordered. "But if there's trouble, drop back and leave us handle it."

Taking the lead, Ysabel pushed through the doors. Following at the Kid's side, Belle looked around in the hope of seeing Tollinger and Barmain. Smoke curled in a billowing cloud beneath the ceiling, but she could see clearly enough. Mexicans and white men, all well-armed, ranged along the bar, dabbled at the various gambling games, or sat drinking around the tables. While coming to the *cantina*, Sam Ysabel had warned Belle of what kind of customers it catered to. The girl read lust, depravity and evil on the majority of the male faces. In one corner, a four-piece band consisting solely of string instruments beat out a fast rhythm to which a girl twirled and gyrated in a high-stepping dance. Other girls of various nationalities, dressed in garish, abbreviated costumes, mingled with the customers.

Unfortunately, as far as Belle could see, the two men she sought were not in the big room.

"Hey, Big Sam!" yelled a voice. *"Cabrito! Saludos, amigos!"*

Even without needing to be told, Belle guessed the identity of the man who was advancing on Ysabel with widespread arms and a welcoming smile that appeared to stretch from ear to ear. Smallish, slender, with a hooked nose above a bristly beard, the man wore clothes in the fashion of a wealthy Mexican *haciendado,* glittering with silver filigree and gold decorative buttons. The deference exhibited by the girls and customers warned Belle that she was looking at Cisco Castro, the owner of the *cantina.*

"Way he takes on, you'd near to reckon he means it," drawled the Kid sardonically in Belle's ear, watching Castro embrace his father around the shoulders. "If he figured he could get away with it, he'd knife Pappy right now."

"It has been much too long since you came here last, Big Sam," Castro stated, stepping back. Then he looked by Ysabel and beamed at the Kid. "And you have grown since our last meeting, *Cabrito.*"

"You ain't, Cisco," the Kid replied.

If Castro felt any resentment at the Kid's barely polite comment, he concealed it. Turning his gaze in Belle's direction, he raked her up and down in the coldly calculating manner of a farmer examining an animal offered for sale. While Castro's lips held a smile, his eyes were cold, expressionless, yet seemed to show a wary, suspicious glint.

"And who is this, Big Sam?" Castro asked.

"Name's Annie," Ysabel answered, without calling Belle forward to be introduced. "Is the bar open?"

"For you, *amigo,* always," Castro enthused, taking Ysabel by the arm and leading him toward the counter.

Instead of following his father, the Kid remained at the door. With Belle at his side, he looked around the room. For a moment, Belle felt embarrassed by the lascivious manner in which several of the men present studied her. Then she noticed that the Kid's gaze had come to a stop. Looking in the same direction, Belle's hope that he had located Tollinger and Barmain met with disappointment.

Two men sat at a small table close to the left side door, but
not the pair that the girl had hoped to see. Dressed in buckskins, they were leathery old Texans; one tall, lean, heavily
bearded and sporting a coonskin cap, the other short, wiry,
with bristle-stubbled cheeks and a large moustache under a
black Stetson hat that had seen better days, months and years.
A Colt revolving cylinder rifle leaned by the taller man's chair
and a heavy-gauge, twin-barreled shotgun rested against the
table close to his companion's right hand. Belle felt certain that
signals of some kind had passed between the Kid and the ancient duo, but figured she had better avoid drawing attention to
the fact. While walking with the Kid after his father, she
glanced again at the pair and found that they were following
her party's progress with their eyes. More significantly, each of
them had picked up his weapon and laid it across his lap.

On reaching the bar, the Kid did not join his father and
Castro. Halting a short distance from them, he took hold of
Belle's arm in his left hand and kept her at his side.

"And what brings you here, Sam?" Castro inquired, indicating the two glasses of tequila poured out by his bartender.

"Pleasure," Ysabel answered, downing the fiery liquor in one
gulp. "And the gal there."

"She is not bad looking, *amigo*. Not bad, if you like them
skinny. With no offense to you or *Cabrito*, of course."

"What's she worth, Cisco?"

"You mean—" Castro breathed, eyeing Belle with fresh interest.

"I mean how much'll you pay me for her," confirmed Ysabel
and saw suspicion flicker to the Mexican's face. "Look, Cisco, I
need me a stake to start smuggling again. And that gal strikes
me as a good way to get it."

"*You* need a stake?" Castro asked.

"Aw hell, Cisco. Don't tell me you've fallen for that story
that me 'n' Lon's got a pile of Yankee gold stashed away. If we
had, would I need to come to you this aways?"

"Of course you wouldn't."

In his life as a *cantina* owner, Castro had bought and sold more than one girl. However, he had never known Big Sam Ysabel to become involved in such transactions. Being suspicious by nature, Castro had been on his guard for a trap. Now he felt that he knew the Big Texan's motive. According to rumors making the rounds, the Ysabel family had hidden away a large sum of money in Yankee gold. By coming to Castro on the pretense of selling the girl, they hoped to convince people that the story was false. Naturally, they had come to Castro, knowing him to be the best market for such merchandise.

"This is something we can't discuss publicly, *amigo,*" Castro declared amiably. "Bring the girl to my office."

"Lon, Annie," Ysabel called, looking their way. "Come with us."

While Ysabel turned his head to speak, Belle saw Castro nod sharply to the attentive bartender. Then she noticed that the Kid, acting as if he were taking a quick glance around the room, gave a slight inclination of his head toward the two old-timers. Again she could not be certain if it was a signal. Neither of them showed any sign of having caught it, if it should be. Instead they continued to sit nursing the shotgun and rifle, drinking their tequila with complete indifference to what was going on around them.

Still holding Belle's arm, the Kid guided her along the bar. They went to the right and Castro opened a door in the wall at the end of the counter. Politely he stood aside for his guests to precede him through it. Going in, Belle darted a quick look across her shoulder. She saw the bartender go through another door behind the counter.

Clearly Castro loved personal luxury and comfort. A thick carpet covered the floor of his private office. In its center stood a large, expensive desk with a highly polished but bare top. For additional furnishings there were a few fancy, upholstered chairs. Big and bulky, a Chubb safe looked almost out of place in a corner of such elegant surroundings. On each wall, heavy drapes hung down to floor level as if covering windows and ensuring the owner's privacy.

"And how goes it, Big Sam?" Castro asked jovially, waving Ysabel into a chair in front of the desk.

"Can't complain," the Texan answered. "How about with you?"

"Things haven't been easy." Castro sighed and sat down facing Ysabel across the desk. "Maybe things will improve now the war is over. Take a seat, *Cabrito.*"

Crossing to the desk, the Kid hooked his rump on to its end at his father's left. The action drew a slight frown from Castro, but he raised no verbal objection to the dark youngster's behavior. Instead he launched into a dirty story, speaking clearly to emphasize its point and, while telling it, darted a look at the wall behind the Ysabels.

Nobody had asked Belle to sit down, so she stood by the door and studied her surroundings. Noticing Castro's interest in the left wall of the room, Belle also turned her attention that way. She had already observed that the desk did not face the door through which they had entered and read significance in its position. As the joke continued, Belle saw the left side drapes stir slightly. It was as if a draft of air had blown briefly through a window. Except that there could be no window behind the drapes. The left side wall was internal, separating the office from whatever rooms lay behind the bar. Remembering Castro's signal and the bartender's departure, Belle began to draw conclusions which she did not like.

After the one quick flutter, the drapes hung motionless. Belle might have wondered if her eyes had played a trick on her, but Castro's attitude hinted that they had not. Sitting back in his chair, the Mexican exhibited an impression of satisfaction like a man who had covered every bet. With the story ended and laughed at, Castro swung his gaze to Belle.

"All right, girl," he said. "Take all your clothes off."

4

CICATRIZ IS A VERY GOOD FRIEND

"How's that?" growled the Kid indignantly, tensing and his right hand moving toward the bowie knife's hilt.

"Didn't you tell *Cabrito* of your intention, Big Sam?" Castro asked nervously.

"Sure I did," Ysabel replied.

"Then surely, *Cabrito,* you and your father have never bought a horse without giving it a thorough examination?" Castro purred. "It is the same now. Come on, girl. Strip yourself so I can see what I'm buying."

"Wha—Why—?" Belle gasped, looking flustered.

"Big Sam is selling you to me," Castro explained. "Didn't he tell you?"

"Like hell he did!" Belle screeched, sounding as coarse and uneducated as might be expected of a girl dressed in such a fashion. With relief, she saw that the Kid had relaxed slightly. "You-all allowed you'd get me work, Sam Ysabel. You never said nothing to me about this."

Until they heard Belle start speaking, the Kid and his father had been on the point of disclosing the real reason for their visit. Seeing Belle's reaction and subsequent behavior, they guessed that she had seen or heard something which had escaped them. So they held their tempers in check and awaited developments.

While speaking, Belle began to sidle across the room. Her hands disappeared behind her back and she wriggled in an embarrassed manner, letting her reticule and parasol fall to the floor. All the time, never looking that way, she edged herself closer to the drapes on the left-side wall. A capable poker player, Ysabel read the signs and prepared to help Belle make her play.

"Shucks, Annie," he said placatingly. "Senor Castro here'll see you right well settled. Do like he says."

"I don't wanna!" Belle protested.

Simulating anger, Ysabel lunged to his feet. Starting toward the girl, he spoke in a harsher tone. The Kid remained seated on the desk, looking over his shoulder at Belle.

"Damn it all!" Ysabel snarled. "You do like you was told, or I'll peel you raw myself."

"Aw, Sam!" Belle whined, backing toward the wall. "It ain't I minds stripping afore you gents. I just don't cotton to these jaspers back of here a-peeking at me."

With that, the girl grabbed at and snatched open the drapes. Doing so confirmed her theory that there was no window behind them. Instead, she exposed a small alcove with a door at its rear end. Inside the opening, three hard-faced Mexicans armed with revolvers formed a living triangle. Spitting out an explosive Spanish curse, the foremost member of the trio lunged forward and lifted his Starr Army revolver to line in Ysabel's direction. In his surprise at being discovered, the advancing Mexican overlooked the fact that somebody other than the big Texan must have pulled open the drapes. He discovered his mistake quickly enough.

Bringing her right hand from behind her back, Belle showed that she had taken apart her parasol and had only dropped its body. As the man burst from the alcove, she raised and slashed down the handle. Out slid the components of the billy. Its ball struck the top of the Starr with a force that ripped the gun from the man's grasp. Nor did his troubles end there. On the heels of the blow, giving its recipient no time to recover, Belle swung her left arm. Her palm caught the center of the man's shoulders, sending him staggering onward. At no time during her attack did she step into sight of the other two Mexicans. After completing their companion's discomfiture, she remained concealed ready to help deal with them when they emerged.

Although as surprised as his men by Belle's actions, Castro recovered quickly and grabbed toward the drawer of his desk. He failed to react quite fast enough. With his suspicions aroused by the girl's actions, the Kid had been ready for something to pop. At Castro's first hostile movement, the youngster swung up his feet and thrust himself into motion. Sliding across the polished top of the desk, he opened his legs and dropped astride Castro's lap. The chair skidded back and crumpled under their combined weights, dumping them onto the floor. Of the two, the Kid came out best from the landing. Before Castro regained his breath, the Kid was sitting on his chest and pricking him under the chin with the point of the bowie knife's blade.

Aware of the type of men Castro hired as bodyguards, Ysabel had no inclination to let the element of surprise slip away from his party. Catching Belle's victim by the front of his shirt, Ysabel brought him to a halt, then heaved him back in the direction from which he had come.

Having seen what had happened to the first man, the other two Mexicans had not tried to rush into the office. Instead, they remained in the alcove and hoped to lure the girl from behind the wall. The hope did not materialize. With their companion hurtling toward them, they found themselves further handicapped. The alcove was not wide enough for them to step aside and let him pass; nor could they shoot at Ysabel without the chance of hitting their colleague. So they compromised by catching the man and shoving him out of the opening. That did not greatly improve their situation. By the time they had cleared the obstruction, Ysabel stood covering them with his big old Colt.

"Tell your boys to yell 'calf rope,' Cisco," Ysabel ordered.

"You best do it," the Kid went on in a caressing voice that sent shivers running through Castro. "If you don't, you'll be too dead to care."

"Put up your guns, *muchachos!*" Castro commanded, knowing that to yell "calf rope" meant to surrender and not doubting for a moment that the Kid would carry out the threat.

Scooping up the first Mexican's Starr, Belle backed to Ysabel's side. She waited until the other two bodyguards had obeyed their employer's order, then turned and strolled over to the desk.

"Let him get up, Lon," she said. "I told you that we couldn't fool a man of Senor Castro's intelligence and should have been frank with him from the start."

Coming to his feet in a lithe movement, the Kid stepped away from Castro and sat on the desk with his legs blocking access to the drawer. Eyes glowing hatred, Castro rose and glared around the office. Suddenly he realized that a change had come over "Annie." She no longer sounded like an uncouth calico cat, but spoke with the accent of a refined Southern lady. Closing her billy into the parasol's handle, Belle smiled in a disarmingly friendly manner at the *cantina*'s owner.

"I apologize for this trouble, *senor,*" Belle declared. "Of course I realize that we made you suspicious and I don't blame you for taking precautions. You aren't hurt, are you?"

"N-No!" The word popped like a cork from Castro's mouth as he stared at the girl and rubbed his rump.

"Get Senor Castro another chair, Lon," Belle ordered and held the Starr to the Mexican. Looking to where Ysabel still covered the bodyguards, she continued, "You can put your gun away, Sam. Senor Castro knows we don't mean any harm and is going to dismiss his men."

"Whatever you say, Miss Belle," drawled Ysabel, returning his Dragoon to its holster. "Now it's your turn, Cisco."

For a moment Castro hesitated. Then his curiosity overrode his anger and suspicion. Much to his surprise, the Kid quit the desk and collected a chair from by the safe.

"Vamos!" Castro snarled at his men and took the revolver from the girl. "Here!" he went on, tossing the weapon to its owner with a gesture of disgust. "Get out of here."

"That's better," Belle stated, after the three bodyguards had left.

Sinking into the chair brought for him by the Kid, Castro studied the girl with interest, but no longer as a prospective buyer. Ysabel and the Kid positioned themselves by the girl and so that they could keep the alcove under observation.

"What's this all about, *senorita*?" Castro inquired.

"Big Sam tells me that you are the best-informed man in the border country, Senor Castro. Is that true?"

"It is," Castro agreed. "There is little happens that I do not know about."

"Then I've come to the right person," Belle told him. "I thought that I had when I first saw you. I need information."

"Then why—?"

"Why did I come dressed like this? To avoid rousing suspicion. For the rest, Big Sam suggested that we pretended he wanted to sell me so that we had an excuse to come and talk privately in your office."

"Ah. So that's why—"

"It was Sam's idea," Belle said depreciatingly. "I doubted if it would work and felt sure that you would see through our deception. That was why I exposed your men—"

"You knew about them?" Castro gasped.

"It seemed a logical precaution for an intelligent man to take," Belle complimented. "That wall was the most likely place for your men to be hiding and I knew you would have more than one man on hand to deal with the Ysabels."

"I see," breathed the Mexican, not hiding the pleasure he felt at Belle's flattering reference to his intelligence.

"Fetch my reticule, Lon," Belle ordered.

"Yes, ma'am," drawled the Kid.

Watching the youngster obey, Castro felt even more intrigued by his female visitor. Any woman—or man for that matter—who could command such obedience from *Cabrito* must be a person of importance. Castro's interest increased when the girl received her reticule. Opening it, she extracted a thick wad of paper money. Staring intently across the desk, Castro saw that the top note was a United States fifty-dollar bill.

"I think Sam suggested that we should act as we did because the information I want concerns one of your friends," Belle remarked, riffling the edges of the bills with her thumb. "He doesn't understand that business and friendship don't mix."

"Which friend would that be, *senorita*?" Castro asked, tearing his eyes from the money with an effort.

"The one called *Cicatriz.*"

"The Scar, huh? And you want to know——?"

"Where he is and what his business is with the two Yankees he met tonight at Orley's saloon."

"*Cicatriz* is a very good friend, *senorita,*" Castro hinted and Belle slid the wad's top bill onto the desk. "Well, maybe not such a *very* good friend." A second bill left Belle's fingers. "But a friend of long standing."

"This long?" Belle inquired, adding the third fifty-dollar bill and ignoring the Kid's low hiss of disapproval.

"Well, not so long perhaps," Castro answered, watching the girl's face.

"Is the friendship dwindling?" Belle wanted to know and the fourth bill joined its companions in front of her.

A shrewd trader, Castro possessed a keen judgment for exactly how much any given market would stand. Unless he missed his guess, the girl had about reached her limit in the bidding.

"It's possible I may have misled you, *senorita,*" the Mexican said, noticing the air of finality with which Belle dropped the fifty bill. He reached toward the money. "Thinking about it, I find that the Scar is unworthy of my friendship."

Laying the handle of her parasol across the bills before he touched them, Belle smiled at Castro.

"I *never* pay for a horse until after I've seen if it is worth the money, *senor,*" she warned.

"Of course you don't," Castro replied, also smiling, if not with his eyes. *"Cicatriz* is taking the two *gringos* to Matamoros tonight. In fact, he has probably already left with them."

"He's more of your friend than I thought." Belle sighed and made as if to gather up the money.

"They will be there for maybe a week!" Castro offered hurriedly.

"Why?" the girl demanded.

"I don't know," admitted Castro. Then, as he saw her lips tighten ominously, he went on, *"Senorita,* I could lie, or make up a reason. But I am dealing fairly with you. *Cicatriz* knows me well. Too well to trust me with much knowledge of his affairs."

Catching Ysabel's eye, Belle saw him nod agreement with Castro's declaration. So she signified her acceptance of the explanation.

"Matamoros's a fair-sized town, Cisco," Ysabel remarked. "So you'll have to narrow it down just a lil mite."

"For two hundred and fifty dollars," the Kid went on, "I'd say it's got to be narrowed down a *big* mite."

"Cicatriz always stays at the *Posada del Infernales,"* Castro elaborated. "That's where you can find him. You know the place, Big Sam?"

"I know it," confirmed the Kid. "Allus sort of reminds me of your place."

"What if he isn't there?" Belle asked.

"There is a rumor that a renegade general is hiring *pistoleros* to help him set up his own republic south of the border. Again I can say nothing for certain, but I think that the Scar may have been finding men to serve him."

"Where's this here general at?" demanded the Kid.

"Rumor says at the fort on the Rio Mendez, between Cruillas and San Fernando," the Mexican replied. "Haven't *you* heard of him?"

"Could've been more'n the one of 'em at it," the Kid pointed out and glanced at the money before Belle.

"And you can tell us nothing more?" Belle asked, guessing what the youngster was thinking.

"I wish I could, *senorita,*" Castro sighed. "As long as *Cicatriz* is in Matamoros, he will stay at the *Posada del Infernales.* As Big Sam and *Cabrito* will tell you, the Scar likes to have friends around him. A man with many enemies must live close to his friends."

"Which same's way ole Cisco here don't stray far from the *cantina,* Miss Belle," remarked the Kid. "Only he's not giving you a whole heap for your money."

"You pay a poor man poorly, Lon," the girl explained. "Senor Castro is rich, so his price is high. But that has its advantages. A poor man would want to make more money and might go to *Cicatriz* and tell him about us."

"Which Cisco wouldn't think of doing?" the Kid scoffed.

"I don't think he will," Belle answered. "For this price, *senor,* I don't expect any warning to reach *Cicatriz.*"

"You have my word as a *caballero,*" Castro assured her, rising and bowing gallantly. Ignoring the Kid's disbelieving sniff, he gathered up the money and dropped it into the drawer of the desk. "And now, if there is nothing more, I must be getting back to my guests."

Belle jabbed an elbow into the Kid's ribs as he opened his mouth to speak. "I'm satisfied, *senor,*" she stated.

Placing the palms of his hands on the top of the desk, Ysabel leaned forward and fixed Castro with his eyes.

"There's just one thing more, *amigo,*" the big Texan said gently. "Miss Belle's toting a fair-sized roll of cash money. Only us four in this room know about it."

"So?" the Mexican said, looking away from where the rest of the money was disappearing into the girl's reticule.

"So if anybody comes round trying to take that money," Ysabel elaborated, "there can't be too many ways to share the blame—if you follow my meaning."

"Pappy's being real polite, him being white 'n' all," the Kid continued. "Me, I'm part *Pehnane* and wasn't learned to talk in circles. So I'm telling you that if we run into fuss 'tween here 'n' where we're going, I'll be coming straight back to tell you all about it. I might even start by tossing a couple of Dragoon balls through them fancy curtains when I come in."

At the reference to his secret, Castro darted an annoyed glare toward the alcove. Following his reaction and guessing at its cause, Belle smiled coldly. Like her companions, she had not been unaware of Castro's avaricious glances at her bankroll. She saw a way of avoiding trouble.

"I don't think we need worry about it happening, *Cabrito,*" she said, exuding quiet confidence. "Any more than Senor Castro need worry about us telling anybody of what we found behind the drapes."

"Like Miss Belle says, Cisco." Ysabel grinned, delighted by the girl's astute grasp of the situation. "If you don't tell, we won't."

"If you *do,*" the Kid purred in his most gentle, therefore most dangerous, tone of voice, "I'll be back."

During the walk across town to the *cantina,* Ysabel had been disparaging in the extreme about Castro's moral standards, but he had also commented favorably on the Mexican's personal courage. So Belle took it as a fitting tribute to the Kid's reputation that Castro showed anxiety at the soft-spoken threat.

All too well Castro knew that the Kid did not speak idly. If an attempt to rob the girl should be made and *Cabrito* came through it alive, he would return to keep his promise. Ensuring that he was killed would not be easy. To organize the attempt would take time and could only be done after the Ysabels had left the *cantina.* On the streets, alert for trouble, they would be difficult if not impossible to surprise. Handled any other way, those making the attempt would pay a dear price. Which raised another point. Finding men willing to go against the Ysabel family would not be easy. Others who had tried it had never succeeded and mostly failed to return. Even Castro's employers might refuse to take the chance.

However, if the Ysabels gave their word that they would keep quiet about the purpose of the left wall's drapes, Castro knew that they could be counted on to do it. So he decided that the loss of the girl's remaining money would be a reasonable price for the protection of a most useful secret.*

"There will be no need for you to return, *Cabrito,*" Castro declared.

The Ysabels and Belle exchanged satisfied glances, knowing that they had made their point.

Waiting until Belle had collected and reassembled her parasol, Castro escorted them from the office. Curious—and a few hostile—stares greeted their return to the barroom, causing Ysabel to lay a hand on their host's sleeve.

"Maybe you'd best come across and see us out, Cisco," the big Texan suggested in a tone that brooked no argument. "That way everybody'll know we're all still *buenos amigos.*"

"If you insist," Castro replied.

"We do," the Kid assured him and Castro yielded to the inevitable.

Once again Belle's personality changed. Hooking her right hand through the Kid's left arm, she became the saloon girl flaunting her delight at being in the company of important men. While crossing the room, she darted glances around. The two old-timers still sat at their table, but no longer nursed their weapons. They gave no hint of being aware of the Ysabel family's departure. Belle wondered if she had been mistaken about the Kid signaling to them.

Outside the *cantina,* Belle's party exchanged mutually insincere expressions of goodwill with Castro and left him. Crossing the plaza, she felt satisfaction at her handling of a delicate situation. After impressing Castro with her ability, she had fed his ego with flattery and made him more susceptible to her request for information. Something told her that the Kid, at least, did not share her high opinion of the affair's outcome.

"I'm not sorry to get out of there," Belle remarked, releasing the Kid's arm.

"We likely wouldn't've if you hadn't guessed about them jas-

---

* While the Ysabel family and Belle kept their promise, the Kid later made use of his knowledge to save his life, as is told in *The Bad Bunch.*

pers behind the drapes," Ysabel replied. "How'd you know about 'em being there?"

"*I* wasn't listening to that dirty story," Belle explained. "So I noticed the drapes move. The rest was easy, especially with the way you played along."

"Figured something was up, way you acted," Ysabel drawled, "and allowed I should set back until I knowed what."

"The thing is, did he tell us the truth about *Cicatriz*?"

"Some of it. Only I'd not count on him playing square with you."

"I don't, Sam," Belle said calmly.

"Then you sure paid high for the bit he told you," growled the Kid. "We could've got that much free after his *pelados* left us with him."

"I doubt it," Belle objected. "And I think it was worth fifty dollars to know where the Scar took Tollinger and Barmain."

"*Fifty?*" the Kid ejaculated. "Either you can't count, or I can't see. I saw you give him—"

"Five fifty-dollar bills," Belle finished for the indignant youngster. "Only four of them are forgeries, printed for us spies to use during the war." Her companions' startled and admiring comments made her smile and she continued, "You surely didn't think I would hand over two hundred and fifty real dollars as easily as all that, did you?"

5

YOU'RE BLOCKING MY TRAIL

"There it is, Miss Belle," the Ysabel Kid remarked, pointing along the street at the *Posada del Infernales*. "We'll soon know if you wasted your money."

"Yes," Belle agreed quietly. "We'll soon know."

"Don't forget what we fixed with Pappy," the Kid warned. "If they're there, we pull out and wait until he's on hand before you take them."

"I'll remember," Belle promised, glancing down at her parasol.

Once more the Rebel Spy had cause to be grateful to the Ysabel family's assistance. They had organized everything so far with smooth efficiency and to her complete satisfaction.

The walk from Castro's *cantina* to Ma O'Grady's house the previous night had been uneventful. On their arrival, Sam Ysabel had told Ma most of what had happened and the woman had helped Belle return her blouse to a state of decorous modesty by stitching back the removed pieces. When Belle had mentioned the two old men, the Kid dismissed them as "a couple of worthless, no-account ole goats' who must have seen the Ysabels someplace or other.

That morning, dressed as a lady again, Belle had accompanied the Ysabels on horseback out of Brownsville. Going upriver along the Rio Grande, they had crossed into Mexico on a small ferryboat which had the advantage of operating in secret. Returning to the ex-consul's residence in Matamoros, the girl had collected her belongings and transferred them to an inn owned by a friend of the Ysabels. There had been two reasons for the change of quarters. Knowing something of her original host's plans for the future, Belle wished to avoid jeopardizing them by starting her vengeance mission from his home. Secondly, the Ysabels felt that the inn would make a better base of operations, being situated in a less high-toned neighborhood than the late Confederate States consulate.

With her wigs and other disguise equipment on hand, Belle had transformed herself into a brassy, flashy blond saloon girl. She felt certain that Tollinger, Barmain and *Cicatriz* would not recognize her.

Then a hitch had developed in their arrangements. A Mexican had arrived at the inn with a message for Sam Ysabel. Having learned in some way of the Ysabel family's return to Matamoros, Don Francisco Almonte wanted to talk with them. A good friend—and supplier of much fine wine before the war —his request had presented the Ysabels with a problem. They were torn between their desire to help Belle and a wish to accommodate Almonte. After some discussion, Belle had offered a compromise. While Ysabel visited Almonte, she and the Kid would scout the *Posada del Infernales* and try to discover whether Castro had told the truth. Ysabel had agreed to the suggestion, but with the proviso that if Belle's enemies should be there, no attempt would be made to tackle them unless he was on hand to help.

Being a sensible young woman, Belle had accepted Ysabel's terms. She believed that the visit to the *posada* could be made without risk of detection. Not only did she wear a disguise, but the Kid dressed differently than on his previous visits to the town. Then he had worn a Confederate States Army uniform, or buckskins. In his black range clothes, he might pass as an ordinary young Texas hard case making a visit to Mexico for private reasons. There seemed sufficient likelihood of it succeeding to make the chance worth taking.

For all her apparent calm, Belle felt the tension rising and seething inside her as she approached the doors of the *posada.* Until she had seen them the previous night, she had forgotten just how deep and bitter her hatred of Tollinger and Barmain was. The memory of their crime had always been with her, but she had pushed it to the back of her mind so that it would not impede her work and chances of survival. Warning herself that she might be headed for a disappointment, she kept walking. Whatever she did, she must prevent her churning emotions from overriding good sense.

"You all right, Belle?" asked the Kid, sensing the mental turmoil that assailed her.

"Yes," the girl replied. "Lon. If I start to do anything *loco,* stop me."

"If I thought you'd do anything *loco,* " drawled the Kid, "I wouldn't go in there with you."

Externally the *Posada del Infernales* resembled Castro's Brownsville *cantina,* being two storys high, made of adobe and timber planks, and dominating the surrounding buildings. The resemblance continued internally, although at that early hour the big barroom was sparsely occupied. Several bored-looking girls sat eyeing Belle with hostility. Behind the bar, a big, fat Mexican leaned his elbows on the counter and scowled at the new arrivals. A few customers were scattered around the room, and in its center four cold-eyed Americans sat in apparent amity at a table with a couple of evil-featured Mexicans. Another Mexican disappeared up the stairs alongside the bar, moving with considerable speed.

All that Belle saw as she and the Kid entered. Then, as they started to cross the room, something attracted her attention. Her eyes went to two familiar figures who were sitting in a corner of the room. Even if she had not been able to see their faces, she would have identified the "couple of worthless, no-account ole goats" from Castro's *cantina.* While other people undoubtedly owned Colt revolving-cylinder rifles and heavy-gauge shotguns, Belle refused to believe that any other hat could attain a state of decrepitude equaling that of the shorter man's Stetson.

"Something up, Annie-gal?" asked the Kid innocently, following the direction of her gaze.

"I smell a rat, Lon Ysabel," Belle replied and realized that the levity had suddenly left her companion. A moment later, she knew why.

Although they did not know it, Belle and the Kid had been under observation as they crossed the street toward the *posada*. There had been three Mexicans with the four Americans, but one of them rose and made for the stairs as soon as he saw the couple. The stockier of the remaining Mexicans pointed through the window and hissed the Kid's name to his companions.

"You sure *that's* him?" demanded a middle-sized, heavily moustached American, his voice a hard New York dialect.

"Si," the Mexican agreed vehemently. "I saw him and the girl come from Villena's *posada* with Big Sam."

"So this's *Cabrito,"* sneered another of the Americans, watching the Kid approach the doors. "He don't look so all-fired savage to me."

"Where is Big Sam?" demanded the remaining Mexican worriedly.

"He went off somewhere," the first Mexican explained. "I think *Cabrito* believes nobody will know him, dressed like that."

"You want him stopping, Yorky?" asked the man who had been unimpressed by the Kid's appearance. In his early twenties, he was tall, well-built and had an air of arrogant toughness. Although dressed in a U.S. Cavalry uniform, it no longer bore official insignia and he carried his Army Colt low on his right thigh in an open-topped, tied-down holster.

"Go to it, Kansas," the middle-sized American replied.

Since their first meeting, Kansas had been set on impressing the other members of the party with his extreme salty toughness. Yorktown Hoxley had known hard men of one kind or another all his life and, like the fabled character from Missouri, needed a visual demonstration before he believed such claims. So he was quite content to let Kansas make the attempt. If the other failed, the remainder of the party could easily settle that baby-faced Texan's hash. Not that Hoxley expected Kansas to fail, having seen the speed with which he could draw and shoot.

Setting down his glass, Kansas nodded toward the bottle of tequila on the table and said, "Fill her up. This won't take long."

With that, he strolled forward and halted deliberately in front of the approaching couple. Hooking his thumbs into his gun belt, Kansas stood on spread-apart feet and a cold, contemptuous grin twisted at his lips. Everything about him rang a warning for the Kid, but it did not cause the Indian-dark youngster to halt or turn aside. Instead, he signaled for Belle to drop back. Disengaging his arm, the girl obeyed. As she prepared to jerk apart her parasol, the Kid walked on with a leisurely seeming stride.

While the Kid did not want trouble, he felt sure that it could not be avoided. As far as he knew, the party to which the man had belonged had no connection with *Cicatriz*. If they did, he would have expected more of them to be facing him. Either way, he would get nowhere by backing down or trying to leave. Unless the Kid missed his guess, that Yankee jasper was spoiling for a fight. In which case, the best thing to do would be oblige him.

"You're blocking my trail, *hombre*," the Kid pointed out, sounding almost angelically mild.

"Then walk round me," Kansas ordered and his right hand lifted to hang above the Colt's butt.

Conversations died away around the room as the girls and other customers realized that something dramatic might soon take place. Belle held the two parts of her parasol in her hands, giving the Kid and his antagonist her whole attention. At Hoxley's table, the Americans watched with interest and the Mexicans fingered their knives. The latter possessed the advantage of knowing *Cabrito*'s hard-earned reputation and lacked their companion's confidence in Kansas.

"I never was no hand at walking," drawled the Kid, continuing his steady advance. "You got something better to offer?"

"Nothing you could take, sonny," Kansas replied. "Tell you, though. I'll let you come by, but the gal stays with me."

"Mister," the Kid said, looking so gentle that butter would be hard put to melt in his mouth, and measuring the distance separating them. "I'd sooner leave her with a hawg!"

Rage twisted at Kansas' face. "Why you—!" he snarled and started to make his draw.

Speaking proved to be an error of tactics. At the first word, the Kid immediately changed from passive relaxation to savage, deadly movement. Gliding forward fast, he ignored the Dragoon. Flashing across his body, his right hand enfolded the hilt of the bowie knife.

To give him credit, Kansas was fast and against most white men he would have achieved his intention. The Kid moved like a *Pehnane* warrior. As the Colt left leather, its hammer drawn back and trigger depressed, the youngster's left hand blurred to slap its barrel outward. Flame ripped from the revolver's muzzle, but the bullet it ejected missed the Kid by inches. At almost the same moment, glinting wickedly in the bar's lights, the great blade of the bowie knife sprang from its sheath to rise outward and across.

Despite his early Comanche training, the Kid did not hold his knife in the Indian fashion with its blade below his fist. Instead he gripped the hilt so that the blade extended before his thumb and forefinger, its razor-sharp edge uppermost. Doing so allowed him to thrust, slash or deliver a backhand chop. He selected the latter method of attack.

To some of the audience, it seemed that the Kid had made a mistake. Striking as he did, the back of the blade would be the part to make contact with Kansas' flesh. The more knowledgeable of the onlookers knew better.

"*A:he!*" grunted the Kid as he struck, giving the traditional Comanche coup cry meaning "I claim it!"

Honed as sharp as the edge, the concave section of the clipped point raked at and bit deep into Kansas' throat. Blood spurted in the wake of the shining steel and the man stumbled backward. Letting his Colt drop, he turned and collapsed onto a table. Coughing out his lifeblood, he slid from there to the floor.

Everything had happened with such devastating speed that even the Mexicans in Hoxley's party sat numbed into immobility for a moment. The Kid's sudden transition from a meek-seeming youngster to a savage Comanche Dog Soldier added to the shock and helped freeze the men at a time when they should have been backing Kansas' play.

Letting out a snarl, Hoxley shoved back his chair and started to rise. His action set an example to the others, causing them to emulate it. Feet rasped on the floor and hands reached weapons as the other members of Hoxley's group tried to stand up.

Transferring his knife from the right hand to the left, in a throw reminiscent of a gunfighter performing the "border shift," the Kid prepared to fetch out his old Colt. Behind him, Belle made a snapping motion with her right hand. The billy opened, its steel ball drawing out the metal rod and coil spring ready for use.

A shot crashed from the right side of the room and the tequila bottle disintegrated on Hoxley's table. Fiery liquor sprayed, intermingled with slivers of glass, peppering the men painfully. Startled curses burst from them, to be cut off on hearing a cracked, irascibly plaintive old voice from the shot's direction.

"Why'd you go and do that for, Cactus?" it asked. "You done sp'iled a good bottle of tee-keely."

Swiveling around still mouthing obscenities, Hoxley jerked his hand away from the butt of his holstered Remington 1861 Navy revolver. Also turning, the rest of the men stiffened and refrained from continuing their hostile movements.

Smoke curled up lazily from the twenty-seven-inch-long, .56 caliber, barrel of the Colt rifle cradled against the taller old-timer's shoulder. That alone did not cause the pacifism displayed by Hoxley's party. The second ancient Texan's shotgun lined disconcertingly in their direction, its enormous eight-gauge twin tubes a fine inducement to compliance.

"Do you reckon I meant to hit the blasted thing, consarn it?" the taller man answered indignantly. "I was aiming at them fellers."

Swinging her eyes from the dying man to the two old-timers, then in the Kid's direction, Belle felt an uneasy sensation of being watched by hostile eyes. Not from the men at the table, whose attention was divided between the young Texan and his rescuers. Instinct guided her gaze in the right direction. At the head of the stairs stood the menacing figure of *Cicatriz*, the gun in his hand lining downward.

Not at the Kid!

With a sensation of shock, Belle realized that the Colt's barrel was slanted in her direction.

Desperately Belle twisted herself aside, and not a moment too soon. *Cicatriz*'s revolver barked and she heard the eerie "splat!" as its bullet plowed a hole through the wide brim of her hat. On the heels of the shot, the Kid completed his draw and the old Dragoon swung up to bellow a reply. Fast taken, his aim proved adequate, if not entirely successful. Propelled by forty grains of prime Du Pont powder—looted from a Yankee patrol during the war—a soft lead, round ball struck the wall after stirring a draft of air before *Cicatriz*'s scarred face. Jerking backward hurriedly, the Mexican disappeared from Belle's range of vision.

Reaching up, Belle jerked off her hat and wig, spinning them aside with the body of her parasol. Then her left hand flew down to pull at the strap securing her skirt. As that garment fell away from her hips, she saw the bartender's fat face twist into lines of anticipatory eagerness and knew that he was doomed to disappointment. Knowing that she might run into trouble, Belle had come prepared to meet it. Under the skirt, she wore skintight black riding breeches and calf-high boots. Although removing the skirt had not left her clad only in undergarments, the skimpy nature of the blouse and figure-hugging fit of the breeches set off her slender, yet eye-catching, contours to their best advantage.

"Let's get him, Lon!" Belle shrieked, racing by Hoxley's party and across the room.

Still holding his bloody bowie knife in his hand, the Kid bounded after the girl. He caught up with her, and they plunged side by side up the stairs.

The occupants of the room watched Belle and the Kid reach the head of the stairs. In the stillness that had fallen after the crashing of the shots, the men and women on the ground floor could hear the girl's and the Texan's feet thudding over the wooden boards of the second story. Suddenly a scream, feminine in pitch, rang out, causing Cactus and Rache to take their attention briefly from Hoxley and his companions.

Seeing his chance, Hoxley took it without hesitation. At any moment members of the French occupation troops policing the city might arrive to investigate the shooting. If that happened, Hoxley had no desire to be asked to explain his presence in either the *posada* or in Matamoros.

"Beat it!" he yelled, heaving over the table in the two old Texans' direction and propelling himself in a leaping run toward the front door.

One of the Americans lunged sideways, right hand fanging toward his gun. In an almost leisurely manner, Cactus swung, lined and fired his rifle. Caught in the head with a .56 bullet, the man's lunge changed to a sprawl and he went down with his revolver unfired.

Pandemonium broke in the *posada*'s barroom. Faced with the possibility that Rache would turn lead loose from his shotgun, the remainder of Hoxley's party showed a quick appreciation of the peril. Ignoring their two fallen companions, they set off after Hoxley as quickly as their legs would carry them.

Girls screeched and screamed, flying like hawk-scared chickens toward the safety offered by the bar. The other customers, although not involved in the fracas, showed an understandable desire to vacate the premises. At such times, the French soldiers were inclined to shoot first and ask questions a good second. In one way the confusion proved a blessing to Cactus and Rache, but in another it was a curse. Various inoffensive bodies interposed themselves between the old-timers and the departing men. So, while they prevented Hoxley's crowd from shooting at the ancient pair, the scattering, darting figures ruined any chance of keeping the fleeing men in the building until the Kid returned. Muttering curses in English, Spanish and Comanche, Rache and Cactus watched the batwing doors swing violently as the four men burst through to the street.

"Shall we go after 'em, Rache?" Cactus inquired and a crackle of gunfire from upstairs supplied the answer.

"Let's go see if *Cuchilo* needs help," Rache answered, setting off in a bandy-legged, but fast, run toward the stairs.

About to follow his companion, Cactus saw the bartender grabbing under the counter for something. Skidding to a halt, the lean oldster swung his rifle up and laid sight on the Mexican's chest.

"Come up empty, Heriberto," Cactus commanded and the man obeyed with alacrity, showing his empty hands as proof of his good intentions.

Reaching the head of the stairs, Belle and the Kid darted along the small passage formed by the outside wall of the *posada* and one of its rooms. Where the room ended, another passage ran at right angles between the front and rear rooms. Halting at the corner, the Kid peered cautiously around. Looking over his shoulder, Belle found the passage to be poorly lighted and deserted. However, a door in the center of the farther side was just swinging shut.

"He's in there!" Belle spat out.

Giving the Kid no time to comment, the girl sprang around the corner and sped along the passage. In her eagerness to reach *Cicatriz* and, if possible, discover the whereabouts of Tollinger and Barmain, Belle paid little attention to her surroundings. Coming to a halt before the door, she took a firmer grip of her parasol handle–billy and prepared to gain admittance to the room. Again she did not wait for the Kid, or let him take the lead. Balancing on her left foot, with its knee flexed slightly, she raised her right leg. Gathering herself as she had learned in *savate* lessons, she propelled her right boot alongside the door-knob with the full power of her gluteus muscles behind it.

With surprisingly little resistance, the door burst inward. Carried on by her impetus, Belle made a discovery horrifying in its implications. No room or floor lay behind the door. Instead it opened onto a gap let into the rear of the building. Twenty feet below, placed so that anybody falling from the doorway could not miss them, a number of sharp-pointed wooden stakes rose upward.

All that Belle saw as she teetered helplessly at the edge of the drop. An involuntary scream burst from her and she tried desperately to keep her balance.

6

I'D SOONER HAD HIM ALIVE

Following Belle, the Kid's keen eyes detected something dangling down the door and across the floor. At first he thought that it might be a strand of cord spun by a spider. Then he realized that no spider he had ever seen could produce a cord of such length and thickness. It might, in fact, be a piece of black cotton thread. Given that much of a doubt, his natural caution and suspicious nature took over. Following the cord to its upper end, he saw that it was fastened to a small hook at the top of the door. That quelled any lingering hope that it had been spun by a spider.

In a flash, the Kid decided that some kind of danger lay beyond the door. Before he could warn her, Belle launched her kick and the terrible peril produced by her action stared them in the face.

Flinging his knife aside, so that its point sank into the opposite wall, the Kid freed his left hand. It flashed up in a continuation of the throw and his fingers closed on Belle's right shoulder. Starting to pivot to the right and pull, he felt his hand slip on the girl's flesh. Then his fingers hooked under the shoulder strap of her blouse. Swinging around, he started to turn and drag the girl away from the sheer drop. The strap broke and the blouse ripped from armpit to waist along its seam, but Belle felt herself drawn to safety. The force of the Kid's pull caused her to release the parasol's handle and it flew along the passage. At the same instant, she became aware of another danger making its appearance.

"Lon!" Belle gasped, staring at the other side of the passage.

A Mexican half-breed holding a knife appeared through a door to Belle's right. Gun in hand, also across the passage, another Mexican sprang out of a room on the left.

Completing his turn, the Kid swung up his Dragoon. From waist high, aimed by instinctive alignment, he touched off a shot. The Dragoon went off an instant ahead of the Mexican's Le Mat, but that proved sufficient. Hurling from the Colt's seven-and-a-half-inch barrel at a velocity of something over nine hundred feet per second, the 219-gram bullet churned into the man's chest. Shock and the force of the impact flung the Mexican backward and his revolver's bullet went harmlessly into the roof. Not for the first time the Kid felt grateful for his decision to retain the heavy old handgun instead of obtaining one of the lighter, more convenient-to-carry 1860 Army Colts. No other handgun of the day packed such stopping power.

Rushing at Belle, the half-breed whipped his knife hand into the air. His appearance of Indian blood showed to an even greater extent in the way he held the weapon. The blade-below-the-hand grip limited the number of ways the knife could be used to a downward chop directed to strike behind the recipient's collarbone and a sidewise stroke aimed at the ribs or stomach.

Ducking her head, Belle flung herself to meet the man. It was an action that took him by surprise, for he was used to more passive or easily frightened women. Belle's head rammed into his belly before he could bring down the knife. With its short-cropped hair, the girl's skull made an effective weapon. All the man's breath burst from his lungs in a croaking gasp and he let go of the knife so that it clattered to the floor without touching its intended victim.

The collision brought Belle and her assailant to a halt, but the girl was ready for it. Wrapping her arms around his knees as he started to bend over her, she exerted all her strength to straighten up. Raising the man into the air, she set his legs free. Passing over her head, he contrived in some way to alight on his feet. Doing so proved to be unfortunate. Combined with the force of Belle's throw, his impetus carried him forward. On his second stride, a realization of his danger struck him. Desperately he grabbed at the jamb of the door, but missed. Nor could he stop. Down came his advancing foot, but no floor was beneath it. Pitching forward, he let out a hideous scream and plunged down to be impaled through the body on one of the stakes.

As her straining muscles were relieved of the man's weight, Belle staggered back a pace. Catching her balance, she turned and struck the wall by the side of the door. With horrified eyes, she watched the man's departure. Hearing the terror-filled cry, the Kid swung around to see what had happened.

Any relief the Kid felt at discovering Belle safe was forgotten. Once more feet sounded in the passage. Looking over his shoulder, the Kid saw *Cicatriz* burst from the room that had harbored the gun-toting Mexican.

"Behind, Belle!" the Kid roared, throwing himself floorward in a rolling dive.

Give her full due, Belle reacted with speed. Even without waiting to see what danger lay behind, she twisted and plunged through the air in the direction of her billy.

Although *Cicatriz* emerged holding his Colt, he found himself faced with a problem. Probably his employers would want him to make sure that the girl died, for they had expressed considerable concern over seeing her the previous night; but he knew that killing her might, almost certainly would, bring about his own death at the hands of *Cabrito*. If he turned the gun in the Kid's direction, the girl would have time to reach her weapon and he had seen the speed with which she tackled the half-breed.

Faced with such a problem, *Cicatriz* decided that his best

solution would be in rapid, immediate flight. Clearly his plans had gone badly astray on both floors of the *posada,* so he gave his attention to saving his own skin.

Learning that the Ysabel family had brought the girl to Matamoros, *Cicatriz* needed little thought to guess why. His employers had mentioned the possibility of her following them during their departure—flight might be a better word—from Brownsville. Nor did the Scar need to exercise his brain greatly to figure out from whom they had obtained information concerning his whereabouts. For a price, Cisco Castro would tell the girl and the Ysabels where to find *Cicatriz.* So the Scar had made arrangements for a watch to be kept on Villena's *posada,* knowing the Ysabel family used it as their headquarters in town.

When his scout had brought the news that Belle and the Kid were on their way, *Cicatriz* had organized a suitable reception. Leaving Hoxley and his men in the barroom to stop the visitors, *Cicatriz* had come upstairs to establish a second line of defense. Maybe all the odds favored the Yankee's party, but with *Cabrito* in the game a man would be a fool to take chances.

An old customer at the *Posada del Infernales, Cicatriz* had access to its secret facilities and prepared to make use of them. With his men positioned in the rooms and his enemies in the *posada,* he had fastened a length of stout black cotton thread to the door of the trap. By pulling on it at the right moment, he had conveyed the impression that somebody had just passed through and closed the door. Although the girl had snapped up the bait, *Cabrito*'s keen eyes and lightning reactions had saved her.

Seeing the trap fail, having been watching through the cracks of their barely opened doors, *Cicatriz*'s companions had made their try and met with an equal lack of success. In the hope of taking the girl and *Cabrito* by surprise, the Scar had made his appearance. Expecting at every moment to feel the Kid's lead rip into him, he tore along the passage ducking and weaving.

Not until he rounded the corner and made for the head of

the stairs did *Cicatriz* recall one very important point. According to his scout, Big Sam had not been with the girl and the Kid. Which raised a serious question.

How had they got by Hoxley's men with so little resistance or opposition?

Looking down the stairs, *Cicatriz* learned the answer. It was all so simple, he should have known—

With an almost bestial snarl of rage, *Cicatriz* started to raise his Colt.

Landing on the floor, the Kid pointed his Dragoon after the fleeing Mexican. Holding down his first inclination to use the revolver as a means of halting *Cicatriz,* he thrust himself to his feet. He doubted if he could aim the four-pound, one-ounce hand cannon with sufficient accuracy to merely bring down and wound the fast-moving, swerving figure. A dead man could not help Belle find Tollinger and Barmain. With that thought in mind, the Kid bounded over and plucked his knife from the wall.

Belle figured out why the Kid did not shoot and marked it as another example of his ability to think straight even in a crisis. Scooping up her billy, she lunged upright. Then she and the Kid started to follow the Scar, watching him turn the corner ahead of them.

A thunderous boom shattered the air, rocking echoes up the stairs and from the walls. *Cicatriz* shot into view, traveling backward so fast that his feet barely touched the floor. His head was a hideous ruin of lacerated flesh, disintegrated brains and shattered bone. Hardened through necessity by more than one contact with sudden, violent death, Belle still could not hold down a gasp of horror. Skidding to a stop, she swung hurriedly away from the ghastly sight of the Scar colliding with and bouncing from the wall, then pitching forward lifeless to the floor.

"Oh God!" Belle gasped.

"Air you-all right, *Cuchilo*?" called a voice.

"Sure," the Kid answered. "Come ahead."

Holding his shotgun, with smoke rising from its left-hand

barrel, old Rache ambled around the corner. He threw a glance at the body, sniffed and turned his gaze to the girl. Concern showed on his seamed, leathery face.

"Right sorry to've done that afore you, Miss Belle," Rache apologized. "Only there warn't no other way with the Scar coming at me, when he'd got a gun in his fist. Anyways, he ain't no loss."

"You did what you had to," Belle answered, still not looking in *Cicatriz*'s direction. "I wonder if Tollinger 'n' Barmain are up here?"

"They ain't showed if they are," the Kid pointed out. "Let's take a look." Nodding toward the gray body, he went on. "I'd sooner had him alive, Rache."

"There ye go!" wailed the old-timer, bristling indignation. "There ye just dod-blasted go! Ain't no suiting you Ysabels, pappy nor button. Whyn't you tell me you wanted him on the hoof and I'd've let him shoot me a couple of times while we was waiting for you to sneak up and rope him."

"Like I told you, Miss Belle." The Kid sighed in patient disgust. "Just a couple of worthless, wored-out ole goats."

"Yah!" Rache sniffed and turned to the girl. "I'm tarnally damned if I can see how come a smart for-real lady like you gotten tied in with these Ysabel varmints, Miss Belle."

"It's the fascination of the horrible," Belle explained, wondering how the old man knew her name.

"That's what it be!" cackled Rache delightedly.

"Where's that other ole fool?" the Kid demanded.

"Down in the bar, keeping ole Heriberto friendly 'n' sociable," Rache explained. "Not that I knows who you're ree-ferring to in them disrespecting words. And didn't you say something about us peeking in the rooms to see if them two fellers Miss Belle's after're hid out there?"

"You're just hoping there'll be a gal with no clothes on in one of 'em," the Kid accused. "Are you up to making a start, Belle?"

Suddenly Belle realized that the exchange of bantering insults had been for her benefit, designed to take her mind off

Cicatriz and the other recent events. A momentary annoyance
bit at her. Despite all her ability, the Kid and Rache still regarded her as a fragile female who needed comforting to prevent an outbreak of hysterics in the face of violent death. Then
her annoyance was replaced by pleasure. The two men, anything but sentimentalists, were deeply concerned about her wel-
fare.

"I'm up to it," she said.

With Rache spluttering furious denials of the Kid's accusation, they commenced the search of the rooms. The brief spell
of flippancy had given Belle time to regain control of her emotions and she was her usual competent self as she accompanied
the Kid.

If Rache had hoped to discover a naked girl during the
search, he was to be disappointed. Every room proved to be
empty, which did not entirely surprise the Kid. He had not
expected Tollinger or Barmain to be present and figured that
the management would remove any possible witnesses in case
the door trap needed to be used. Cleaning his knife's blade on
the blankets of the last room's bed—which did not make them
much dirtier—the Kid sheathed it and returned the Colt to its
holster. Then he and the girl joined Rache in the passage and
delivered their negative result.

"Same with me," the old-timer admitted. "Now we'd best
conclude to get the hell out of here. I just saw a bunch of Frog
puddle-splashers headed this way."

"How far off?" Belle demanded.

"Along the street a piece. Only we can't get out and away
afore they come."

"Then we'll have to try something else," the girl declared,
leading the way downstairs. "Not by fighting, either, unless
we're forced to do it."

"Let's hope somebody's got something else in mind, then,"
drawled the Kid.

"I just may have at that," Belle admitted, thinking fast.

On reaching the ground floor, they found Cactus seated on
the bar with his rifle across his knees. The Army Colt revolver

from his belt holster was pointed in the general direction of Heriberto's fat stomach. Several girls were peering through the half-open door behind the counter, having gone through it into the room beyond when the trouble started. Apart from them, the barroom was empty.

Darting across the room by the two bodies, Belle grabbed up her skirt. The Kid and Rache joined Cactus at the bar and they waited to hear what the girl planned to do. Swiftly she donned her skirt and fastened it into place. Collecting her wig, the hat and the body of the parasol, she returned to the counter. While the Kid assembled the parasol, she replaced the wig and placed the hat on at a rakish angle. During the search of the upstairs rooms, she had managed to fasten her broken shoulder strap. Pulling it apart again, she allowed the blouse to trail around her waist. Throwing a look at the doors, to estimate how much time she had, Belle swung back to the Kid.

"Slap my face hard!" Belle ordered.

"Wha—?" the Kid ejaculated.

"Do it, damn you!" Belle hissed. "I'm your wife, kidnapped by the men you killed and you've come to rescue me. Now slap me hard. *Pronto!*"

Such was the vehemence in the girl's voice that the Kid dropped the parasol and obeyed. Whipping around his right hand, he lashed its palm across Belle's face. The force of the slap rocked her head over and left livid finger marks on her cheek, bringing tears to her eyes.

Screwing up her face to keep the tears coming, Belle ruined her already smeared makeup and mussed up the hair of the wig. Then, hearing the sound of heavy boots outside, she thrust herself up close to the Kid.

"Hold me!" she commanded, wrapping her arms around his neck. "Come on. Don't tell me this's the first time you've done it with a girl?"

"I never had to hit her first," the Kid answered, cradling Belle's slender torso up to his chest.

The door burst open. Followed by six privates armed with rifles, a burly French infantry sergeant entered warily. Coming to a halt, gripping a Lefaucheux revolver, the sergeant scowled at the two bodies. Then he raised his eyes and studied the group at the bar. Cactus had already jumped from his perch and holstered his Colt, to stand close to where the Kid was holding Belle in his arms. Slightly clear of the others, Rache rested his shotgun's barrels in a casual-seeming manner on top of the counter. Maybe it looked that way to the French soldiers, but Heriberto knew that the twin tubes aimed straight at him.

"What's all this?" demanded the sergeant in passable English and walking over to look at the dead men.

"It's on account of me granddaughter here," Cactus replied, indicating the sob-shaken shoulders of the girl. "Them fellers done stole her offen our ranch over in Texas."

"We come to take her back peaceable," Rache went on, without diverting his attention or weapon from Heriberto. "Only them fellers wouldn't have it that way. Caught 'em roughing her up some tearing her clothes 'n' all. Had to kill some of 'em a mite to make 'em quit it."

Stepping by the corpses with the air of finding them unimportant, the sergeant approached the bar.

"Is that what happened, you?" he snarled at the bartender.

Maybe Heriberto had no love for the Kid's party, but he possessed an even greater antipathy toward the European invaders of his country. Not for patriotic reasons, but because they had disrupted his trade and reduced his *posada*'s once considerable takings to a fraction of their original worth. More than that, Rache's shotgun menaced his existence and the old-timer's eyes flashed a grim warning that the bartender took to heart.

"Si, Senor General," Heriberto lied, but with an expression of pious honesty that might have fooled his mother. "They treat her very cruel."

"Gal's my wife, sergeant," the Kid said, loosening his hold so that Belle could turn her reddened, tear-streaked face to look plaintively at the Frenchmen. "You don't hold what I done again' me, do you?"

"I don't," the sergeant admitted as a low murmur of pity and

condolence rose from his men. "But you'd better leave Matamoros as quickly as you can."

"You can count on it, sir," Cactus promised and, having had
some experience with French noncommissioned officers, dipped
a hand into his pants pocket. "Say, can we buy you 'n' your
men a drink to show there's no hard feelings and how sorry we
be?"

"We can't drink on duty, and a sergeant never drinks with
his men," replied the noncom and winked. "But if you let me
have the money, I'll see that we all drink your good health
later."

"Anyways you want it, Sergeant," said Cactus obligingly,
producing and handing over a U.S. ten-dollar piece.

Accepting the money, the sergeant thrust it into his pocket
with such an air of ownership that it seemed doubtful whether
his subordinates would ever taste the drinks or toast the giver's
health.

"This is a bad place to be in," the noncom warned the Texans. "You had better take the girl back to your home."

"We'll do that," Cactus agreed. "Only we'll stay put a spell if
it's all right with you. Until she's settled a mite."

"You can do that," the sergeant confirmed and glared at
Heriberto. "See my friends come to no harm, you fat pig. And
don't throw this carrion into the street or I'll come back and
tear your guts out with a bayonet."

"*Si, Senor General,*" the bartender whined.

"And don't let there be any more trouble in this den of
thieves," the sergeant warned, before turning on his heel and
telling his men to leave.

"Keep acting like you're real worried about me, Lon!" Belle
whispered, feeling the youngster's arms relax as the soldier
marched toward the door.

Gambling on the French soldiers being indifferent to trouble
that involved only Americans and Mexicans had paid off. Belle
had known enough about the occupying troops to have felt sure
that they would not be overzealous in their duties of policing
the town. So her plan had worked. However, she did not wish

to ruin their advantage by actions that might arouse the sergeant's suspicions.

"There now, Annie-gal," the Kid said loudly, in what he hoped would sound a consolatory manner. "Don't you go fretting no more. It's all done with now."

"That's what you think, Lon Ysabel," Belle warned *sotto voce*, watching the soldiers pass through the batwing doors.

"How do you mean?" the Kid wanted to know.

"I think you enjoyed slapping my face," Belle explained with mock grimness, "because of what happened in Castro's office last night."

7

I'D GO THROUGH HELL TO GET THEM

Releasing the girl after the soldiers had left the *posada,* the Kid looked at her and asked worriedly, "Did I hurt you?"

"No more than that female pugilist I had to fight in New Orleans,"* Belle answered, wryly fingering her cheek.

"Did you lick her?" Rache inquired.

"Finally," Belle admitted. Then she swung to face the bartender and her voice hardened. "Where are the two *gringos?*"

Heriberto looked at the girl with interest and some trepidation. Despite the tear-smeared makeup and gaudy, if disheveled, clothes, that was no ordinary saloon worker. Everything about her, the way she had acted since her arrival, her voice and deportment, the respect she obviously commanded from the three Texans, warned him of that. There was a grim determination about her, the air of a person used to being obeyed and capable of enforcing obedience.

Wanting to avoid answering the question, or to prevent anybody knowing of it should he be forced to do so, the bartender turned and snarled at the watching girls. Even after they had

* Told in *The Rebel Spy.*

retreated and closed the storeroom door, he felt that some evasion ought to be attempted.

"They ran out after you went upstairs, *senorita. All* of them that could."

"I mean the two who *Cicatriz* worked for," Belle elaborated coldly.

"Quién sabe?" Heriberto answered. "I don't—"

"Go and call the French sergeant back, *Cabrito,"* Belle ordered. "Tell him that we think this fat one hired the men who kidnapped me."

"No!" Heriberto yelped, realizing what his fate would be if the sergeant returned. Having received ten dollars, he would regard himself under an obligation to help the givers. "I don't know where they are, *senorita."* He crossed himself fervently. *"Madre de Dios!* I tell you the truth."

"Have they been here?" Belle demanded.

"Only once, *senorita.* Last night, late. They came with *Cicatriz,* looked around and didn't like what they saw. So they left and haven't been back."

"Why didn't *Cicatriz* go with them?"

"He went, but came back, *senorita.* Maybe they're staying at some place that wouldn't have the Scar inside."

"Which'd be nigh on every place in Matamoros 'n' Brownsville," Rache growled. "I hates to talk ill of the dead, but that's the only way with *Cicatriz."*

"What did *Cicatriz* want with the two *gringos?"* Belle asked, making adjustments to her torn blouse so that it would serve her during the return to Villena's *posada.*

Sweat trickled down Heriberto's fat face and he ran the tip of his tongue across lips that suddenly felt dry. Discussing the customers' affairs had never been a sound business policy, especially when considering the type of trade attracted by the *Posada del Infernales.* Refusing to do so could prove equally dangerous and painful when dealing with *Cabrito* or his two ancient *compañeros.*

"He was to help them hire men, *senorita,"* the bartender replied, having concluded that his present company posed a greater threat than the two *gringos* who had employed *Cicatriz.* "The *americanos* your *amigos* ran out of here were some of them."

"Who were they hiring for?" Belle demanded.

"They said for the French general at the fort on the Rio Mendez," Heriberto answered.

"Why'd a French general want to hire guns?" Rache grunted.

"I don't know," Heriberto whined and cringed away as if expecting a blow or worse to repay his lack of knowledge.

"He's telling the truth," Belle stated after scrutinizing the Mexican's face. "I shouldn't have expected to find Tollinger and Barmain here. Their kind are all for equality, but not to the extent of living among what they regard as the lower classes. We may as well get going."

Cradling his shotgun on the crook of his left arm, Rache eyed Heriberto as if disappointed that he had not needed to use it. Cactus gathered up his rifle and the Kid handed Belle her parasol. Then they left the *posada,* followed by Heriberto's hate-filled scowl.

"Want for me to stick around, hide out, in case they come looking for *Cicatriz?*" asked the Kid.

"It wouldn't be safe, Lon," Belle objected. "Not unless you change your clothes. Dressed like a *peon,* you might get away with it. We'll see what Big Sam thinks first."

"Why don't me 'n' Rache nose around a mite and see if we can find where they're living, Miss Belle?" suggested Cactus.

"That's an idea," Belle agreed. "Unless they're at the U.S. consulate, they're likely to be at one of the better hotels."

"We got friends in 'em all," Rache stated.

"Emptying the spittoons 'n' washing out the chamber pots," finished the Kid.

"These gentlemen mean *their* friends," Belle pointed out, "not yours. And you might introduce us. Somehow you never got around to doing it last night."

"I never thought anybody'd want to know 'em," drawled the

Kid. "Ain't no telling what foolishness women'll want. This here's Cactus Jones and Hor—Hor—"

"Horatio Charles Wilberforce, ma'am," Rache put in, blazing with exasperation. "Blasted young pup done forgot me name!"

"With a name like that, it's best forgot," scoffed the Kid. "Anyways, that's who they are, Belle, for what it's worth."

"When I asked about them last night," Belle pointed out accusingly, "you told me—"

"I was just showing you that it's not only she-male spies, can play sneaky," grinned the Kid. "And who'd want to admit they knowed a couple of ornery, mean ole goats like them?"

"He means us, Miss Belle," Rache informed the girl sadly. "Danged *Pehnane,* never did have no ree-spect for age, wisdom, nor beauty."

"You're sure old," admitted the Kid, "but nobody'd give you claim to the other two."

"Ignore him, Horatio," Belle ordered, taking the old-timer's arm. "*I* know you're both perfect gentlemen. Not like some of the youngsters you meet these days. Why I bet neither of you would slap a lady's face."

"They wouldn't," the Kid agreed with reservations. "Not less'n she was a whole heap smaller than them."

Despite the levity of their conversation, Belle and her companions kept a careful watch around them as they walked away from the *Posada del Infernales.* There were a few details the girl wished to have cleared up, so, with wrathful interruptions from Rache at the derogatory comments aimed his way, the Kid satisfied her curiosity.

While Cactus and Rache had been friends with the Ysabel family for several years, the Kid's signal had prevented them from coming over and speaking the previous evening in Castro's *casino.* Instead, they had kept clear, but were ready to lend support should it be needed. On Belle's party leaving, the old-timers had stayed behind to guard against pursuit by Castro's employees. None had come, so they finally followed the girl and the Ysabels to Ma O'Grady's house.

Arriving after Belle had retired for the night, Cactus and Rache had learned her identity. On being told of her vengeance mission, they had insisted on offering their services. There followed a brief, irate and profane string of objections by Rache to the Kid's libelous statement that only blackmail persuaded him to come along. Being assured by Belle that she did not believe a word of the story, but agreed with Rache's comments on the Kid's morals, the old man permitted the explanation to continue.

Crossing the Rio Grande at sundown, Cactus and Rache had reached the *Posada del Infernales* some time before Belle and the Kid arrived. Mingling with the other customers, they had avoided drawing attention to themselves until the appropriate moment to make their presence felt.

"And I'm pleased that you were there," Belle told the old-timers at the end of the recital.

"Company you was keeping, I ain't see-prised," Rache snorted, eyeing the Kid malevolently and strutting like a bantam cock with the girl on his arm.

"Ain't it time you pair was headed off around them hotels as is full of all your rich friends?" demanded the Kid.

"It is," agreed Cactus. "Happen I can pry Rache offen Miss Belle's arm, we'll get to going."

"Way some ornery young cusses slap her around, I figured she needed pertecting," Rache explained, relinquishing the girl's arm with an air of reluctance. "You let me know happen he does it again, ma'am, and I'll whup him good."

Watching the two old-timers amble off along a side street, Belle smiled.

"They're real nice people, Lon."

"Yes'm. And don't let all that bluster fool you. They're a couple of forty-four-caliber men."

Belle had heard the term before and knew it to be one that a Texan did not award lightly.* Continuing her pose as a saloon girl, she hooked on to the Kid's left arm and strolled at his side

* How the name came into being is told in .44 Calibre Man.

until they reached Villena's *posada*. Entering the building, they found that Sam Ysabel had just returned. When they joined him in the deserted dining room, he looked them over sardonically.

"You run into fuss, boy?" Ysabel inquired.

"Some, Pappy. Rache had to kill *Cicatriz.*"

"I'll buy him a drink for it. Were they with the Scar, Miss Belle?"

"No," Belle replied, trying to conceal her disappointment.

"Rache killed him afore we could ask about it," the Kid explained. "Couldn't do nothing else, though."

"Where're Rache 'n' Cactus now?" asked Ysabel.

"Making the rounds, seeing if they can learn where them two soft-shells're at," the Kid replied. "What'd Don Francisco want, *ap'*?"

"I'll go and change," Belle offered, thinking that Almonte's business with the Ysabels might be private.

"Like you stay on, Miss Belle. You can maybe help some," Ysabel requested and nodded to the nearest table. "Let's sit a spell, talking's easier that way." After they had taken seats, he continued, "Don Francisco wants our help, Lon."

"That figures," drawled the Kid. "Only Belle don't know who he is."

"He's fighting for Juárez," Ysabel explained. "I reckon you know how things are down here, Miss Belle."

"I know a little about them," Belle corrected, for the conditions existing in Mexico, and their causes, were extremely complicated.

Basically, throughout their years of civil conflict, the Conservatives under *Presidente* Miramón and the Constitutionalists led by Benito Juárez had financed their respective war efforts by extracting forced contributions from foreign businessmen and property owners. Enraged by continued outrages and abuses of its nationals, the United States Congress had withdrawn its recognition of Miramón's government in 1858. Two years later, receiving moral and material aid from north of the border, Juárez had been able to take the offensive. Before the

War Between the States had brought an end to the United States' assistance, he had defeated the Conservatives. On assuming office, he had expelled the Spanish minister, the papal legate and various members of the episcopate.

Faced with legitimate debts to various European countries totaling some eighty-two million dollars, the Mexican Congress had voted to suspend paying even the interest due on the money for at least two years. That had played into the hands of the ambitious Napoleon the Third. Desiring to establish a French colony in America, he had negotiated a convention between his country, Great Britain and Spain to enforce demands for payment.

When Napoleon's true purpose had become obvious, the British and the Spaniards had withdrawn their support. Pouring more French troops into Mexico, Napoleon had sought other allies. By arranging a fake Mexican plebiscite that offered to make Maximilian —brother of Emperor Francis Joseph— the country's ruler, Napoleon had obtained support and reinforcements from Austria, Belgium and Turkey. Driven from office, unable to match the superiorly equipped European invaders in open battle, Juárez now fought a guerrilla war to try to free his homeland.

"Thing being," Ysabel said, "everybody down here wants to know what the Yankees'll do now the war's over."

"That's understandable," Belle admitted, removing her hat and wig.

The fate of Mexico might depend on which side the United States gave its support. During the war, the Federal government had tried to steer a central path and avoid antagonizing either side. With a cessation of hostilities north of the Rio Grande, both the French and Mexican authorities would be waiting anxiously to discover what the reformed United States' policies were going to be.

"What do you reckon, Miss Belle?" asked Ysabel.

"I reckon that you should stop calling me 'Miss,'" Belle replied, wanting a moment's grace to assemble her thoughts. "It makes me feel awful old."

"I'll mind it," Ysabel promised. "Seeing's Lon's stop doing it already."

Ignoring the incongruous sight she must present with her facial makeup ruined and general bedraggled appearance, Belle thought for almost a minute before she replied to the big Texan's question.

"You remember why we were sent to General Klatwitter, Sam?"

"Yes'm."

Belle's last, abortive mission had been a final, desperate throw of the dice for the South. On the verge of defeat before the Union's superior numbers, arms, equipment and economy, the Confederate government had hoped that the renegade general's intervention would prolong the war. Already in the North, public opinion had been growing more and more vociferous in its demands for an end to the hostilities. So the possibility of being compelled to continue the struggle might have caused the Union's Congress to offer peace while the South was still in a position to bargain for terms. General Grant's rapid advance and successes, along with Belle's unavoidable failure to complete her assignment, had prevented this from happening. It was a factor to be taken into consideration.

"I don't think that the Union government will be willing to commit themselves yet," Belle went on. "Right now, everybody up North is sick of war with its death, losses, miseries and increased taxations—"

"Knowing Yankees," interrupted the Kid, "that last'll bother 'em most."

"Keep mum and hear Mi—Belle out," his father ordered.

"If you don't, I'll sic Rache onto you," Belle warned, then became serious. "Congress won't want to give active support to either side until the voters have forgotten how much fighting the South has cost them. So I think they'll try to avoid becoming involved. Being drawn into another war could sweep them out of office."

"That's about how Don Francisco sees it," Ysabel admitted soberly.

"Then what's bothering him?" Belle inquired. "Surely the *Juáristas* didn't believe that the Yankees would come marching straight down here to help them against the French now the war is over?"

"Some of them might have, but Don Francisco figures the same as you."

"Then—?"

"It's that French general down on the Rio Mendez—"

"I don't follow you, Sam," Belle stated. "If he's trying to establish a private republic, it will weaken the French's fighting strength. And there's not much chance of him bringing it off."

"Likely not," agreed Ysabel. "Only it'll weaken the *Juáristas* some as well. You know there're fellers fighting for ole Benito who don't exactly cotton to his ways 'n' notions?"

"The big landowners, you mean?"

"Nope. Maybe some of them don't cotton to a Zapotec Injun being *el presidente,* no matter how smart he is. But mostly they figure he'll play square with 'em if he wins."

"Then who—?"

"Don Francisco reckons it's the soft-shells. *They* allow Juárez'll be too easy-going on the *haciendados.* Them's the sort this renegade general's likely to be drawing, along of some of the *bandidos* who ain't making enough loot fighting the French."

"I see," Belle breathed. "And they're willing to throw in with this general to bring Juárez down?"

"Something like that," agreed Ysabel. "Anyways, Don Francisco wants us, Lon 'n' me, to go down to this fort and learn who's in the deal, how strong they are, what they're fixing to do, and such."

"Don Francisco knows the general is hiring gunfighters," Belle guessed. "So he wants you to go there pretending to be looking for work."

"That's about the size of it," Ysabel admitted.

Sitting back in her chair, Belle studied the dark, expressionless features of the big Texan. All too well she could imagine his dilemma. He had promised to help hunt down the murderers of her parents and now found himself faced with the possibility of having to refuse an old friend's request for assistance. Yet Belle wondered if the two problems might be compatible.

"*Cicatriz* was helping Tollinger and Barmain to gather men for this general," the girl said quietly.

"Or so we got told," growled the Kid.

"*Twice,*" Belle reminded him. "I think that we heard the truth. The thing is, why are they doing it?"

"We could maybe try asking 'em," the Kid suggested. "Only we can't find 'em to do it."

"Rache and Cactus might attend to that for us," Belle pointed out. "If not, the fort on the Rio Mendez would be a good place to start looking for them."

"You reckon that's where they're going, Mi—Belle?" asked Ysabel. "They might be hiring help for Juárez and making out it's to fight for this General Caillard so nobody'd know."

"That's possible," Belle admitted. "It might account for why they didn't tell the patrol in Brownsville who I was, or help to chase me. They wouldn't want to have to explain how they knew me as it might arouse suspicions about their reasons for being on the border. They wouldn't want it even suspected that members of the Yankee Secret Service were becoming involved in Mexican affairs."

"Ole Benito don't have much money," the Kid pointed out. "And them jaspers we locked horns with weren't the kind to fight for free."

"There's that to it," Belle agreed. "But if Don Francisco's right about the renegade attracting soft-shells, Tollinger and Barmain might be going to help their own kind; perhaps without official sanction."

"You mean they might not be Yankee spies no more?" asked the Kid.

"They might not. In which case, they're acting on their own. I think that we should go to this fort, Sam. How far is it?"

" 'Bout eighty miles south, along the coast."

"Two days' ride. Unless we find them in Matamoros, I suggest that we go to the fort and look for them."

"What if they're not there?" the Kid wanted to know.

"Then we'll do as Don Francisco asks, come back and report and start looking again," Belle replied. "Should we find them here, I'll still come along to the fort, if you'll have me."

"We'd admire to have you along, M—Belle," Ysabel began.

"You're improving." Belle smiled. "You almost didn't say it that time—But what?"

"Huh?" grunted Ysabel.

"We'd admire to have you along, but—" Belle elaborated. "That's what you intended to say."

"Damned if I could ever stand smart woman." Ysabel grinned. "I don't know what kind of jasper this Caillard is, but I can figure out the sort of fellers who'll be gathering round him."

"So can I," Belle answered. "Malcontents, deserters from both sides, plain thieves after loot."

"As mean 'n' ornery a bunch of cutthroats and *pelados** as you could ask to miss meeting," Ysabel confirmed. "I'd hate to take a for-real lady like you among 'em."

"If Tollinger and Barmain are there, I'll chance it," Belle said quietly. "I'd go through hell to get them!"

The cold, grim, deadly determination in the girl's voice warned her audience that she would not be swayed from her purpose by any arguments or warnings of possible danger.

* *Pelado:* used in this context it means a grave- or corpse-robber of the lowest kind.

8

LET'S GO IN OVER THE WALL

"There she be," announced Horatio Charles Wilberforce, pointing through the deepening dusk as he sat his wiry dun horse alongside Belle's *bayo-cebrunos** gelding on the second day after her visit to the *Posada del Infernales*. His entire attitude seemed to claim that he was responsible for what lay before them.

Despite their excellent sources of information, Rache and Cactus had failed to locate Belle's enemies. The short oldster had complained bitterly over the failure, claiming that he or Cactus should have followed the hard cases when they fled from the *posada,* until Belle pointed out that both of them had been needed more urgently inside the building. As it was, they had found the hotel at which Tollinger and Barmain had been staying, but reached it too late. According to their friend at the hotel, a Mexican had arrived and asked to see the two Yankees. Whatever he had told them caused the pair to pack their bags and leave hurriedly. Continuing their investigations, the old-timers discovered that the objects of their search had not taken

---

* *Bayo-cebrunos:* a dun color, shading into smoky gray.

rooms in another hotel. So they had visited the United States consulate. Contacting a Mexican friend employed by the consul, they again drew a blank. Tollinger and Barmain were not in residence with their government's representative.

Dressed as a *peon,* the Kid had scouted the *Posada del Infernales.* He had returned to report that neither Tollinger and Barmain nor the Yankee hard cases were present. Further inquiries had brought to light that Hoxley had taken his men out of Matamoros, but the informant could not say if Tollinger and Barmain had accompanied them.

By that time, it had been too late to think of setting after the men that day. Instead, Belle's party had made their preparations to leave the following morning. The girl found that she would have four companions to back her on arrival at Fort Mendez. As Rache had put it, no self-respecting Texas gentlemen could contemplate entrusting a lady of quality to them shiftless Ysabel varmints, so he and Cactus intended to go along.

The Ysabels had obtained the *bayo-cebrunos* gelding for the girl to ride, claiming it to be a horse with *brio escondido*—hidden vigor, or stamina of a high order—and ideally suited to her needs. In addition, they had produced a sturdy packhorse to carry the items Belle felt might be of use on her mission. For the journey, she wore her boots, riding breeches, a dark blue shirt and a black Stetson. Butt forward in a fast-draw holster on her right thigh hung the ivory-handled Navy revolver presented to her by the Dance Brothers, Texas firearms manufacturers, as a tribute to her services in the Confederate cause.

Starting early the next morning, Belle's party had headed south. All her companions were well-mounted: the Kid on a magnificent big white stallion that had a nature as wild and savage as his own; Sam Ysabel was afork a large *grulla* stud the mousy-gray color of a sandhill crane; Cactus sat a leggy, saffron-hued *bayo-azafranados* gelding; Rache's dun looked as small, wiry and aggressive as its master. They rode low-horned, double-girth Texas range saddles, with bedrolls fastened to the cantles and their shoulder arms in the boots. In such company,

Belle had reason to be grateful for her mount's *brio escondido* qualities. She also found satisfaction in the Texans' unspoken approval of her riding skill.

Soon after leaving Matamoros, ranging ahead of the others, the Kid had found hoof tracks of approximately the right age to have been made by the hard cases' mounts and going in a southerly direction. There had been at least six horses, which might mean that Tollinger and Barmain had accompanied Hoxley's bunch.

Discussing the discovery, Belle and her companions had decided against increasing their speed in an attempt to catch up with the other travelers. The group ahead might not be the men from the *Posada del Infernales,* and even if they were, the lead they had built up could only be reduced by pushing the horses very hard. So Belle and the Texans had concluded that their best plan would be to follow at a pace which would leave their mounts with a reserve of stamina to meet the needs of any emergency.

Covering almost forty miles that day, they had made a comfortable but carefully concealed camp at sundown. Before turning in for the night, Belle had formulated a plan to cover the eventuality of her enemies' having already made contact with the renegade general. Explaining her scheme to the Texans, she found that they considered it worth trying if the circumstances should permit. At dawn they had ridden on and at last, with the sun again sinking in the west, had come into sight of their destination. Keeping back among the trees on the fringes of a large *bosque,* they examined their surroundings with interest.

One aspect of the affair had been puzzling Belle, but she could now see the possible answer. With so many people involved in it, the French high command must have heard rumors of General Caillard's defection. So Belle had wondered why no steps had been taken to deal with him. Looking ahead, she could understand the reason for the French's inactivity.

Built by men who had unlimited cheap labor and adequate materials at their disposal, the fort nestling in a bend of the Rio Mendez was an impressive structure. Through embrasures cut into the twenty-foot-high stone walls, heavy muzzle-loading cannon mounted *en barbette* covered all the approaches. Belle counted four such guns on each wall and guessed that they would be at least forty-two-pounders.

While the builders had not troubled to surround the walls with a water-filled moat or a deep ditch, or to provide an outlying earthwork demilune, the place was still formidable. An attacker would be compelled to send his men from any side across almost a mile of level, open ground under fire from the cannon and rifles on the terreplein. Assuming that there was an internal water supply—which seemed likely—and adequate provisions, a determined garrison could only be evicted by a fully organized and equipped siege. Even then, capturing the fort would be anything but easy. In fact the French had gained control of it only through the Mexican commandant betraying his trust and handing it over. Probably Maximilian's high command did not believe the effort of recovering it justified the high price in lives, material, time and effort that they would have to pay.

Producing field glasses from their saddle pouches, Belle and Ysabel studied the fort. They could see sentries patrolling the walls. Five in all. Two on the side facing them, working outward from the main gates, and one on each other wall. Inside there would be quarters for the garrison, stables, storerooms, an underground magazine and, possibly, accommodations for wives. All that showed above the walls was the roof of a large building in the center of the enclosure, corresponding with the keep of an old-time castle.

"Look up there!" the Kid remarked, pointing.

Following the direction he indicated, the others saw a small group of riders coming downstream along the banks of the Rio Mendez. Through her glasses, Belle found them to be Mexicans, led by a tall, swarthily handsome man dressed elegantly but with cruel lines to his features. He and his companions were well armed and superbly mounted.

"Well, I'll swan!" Ysabel breathed, also using a pair of battlefield "liberated" glasses. "If that ain't Ramon Peraro, I'll vote Republican."

"Mean ye don't?" Rache sniffed, squinting at the newcomers.

Recalling comments made by the Ysabels during her last assignment, Belle frowned. Ramon Peraro led a particularly ruthless *bandido* gang and he came from a family that had always been prominent in Mexican criminal circles.* Also, he might have reason to dislike her companions.

"Looks like his arm's done healed up," the Kid remarked.

"I wonder if he really knows what happened the day he was wounded?" Belle said soberly, lowering her glasses. "Have you heard anything, Cactus, Rache?"

"Only how him and the late Bully Segan locked horns, which's how Bully comes to be 'the late,' " Cactus replied. "Do you know something about it, Miss Belle?"

"It was all Lon's fault," Belle replied.

"It mostly is," grunted Rache, before she could continue her explanation.

Trying to stop Belle reaching General Klatwitter, members of the Yankee Secret Service had spread the story among the various border gangs of how much money she was carrying. Learning that the Peraro and Segan bands intended to cooperate in an attempted theft, the Kid had stolen some of the latter's horses in a way that laid suspicion on the former. In the fight that followed, Segan died and Peraro had received a wound which prevented him from continuing the hunt for Belle's party.

"Could be that none of 'em knowed for sure what did happen," the Kid said. "They'd not seen me around. Thing being, what's Peraro doing here?"

"Come to see if this Frog general's worth joining, likely," Rache guessed. "His kind drop down like buzzards if there's a smell of easy money."

"It looks like they're expected," Belle put in, whipping up

---

* And still are, as is told in *Point of Contact* and *Run for the Border*.

her glasses as the huge double gates swung open and Peraro's band rode through.

"There's a fair slew of horses inside," Ysabel commented. "McClellan saddles, dinner-plate rigs, a few with just blankets. I'd say they'd got visitors."

"So would I," Belle agreed, following the significance of the statement.

Most Union and Confederate cavalry regiments used the McClellan-pattern saddle and many of them must now be in civilian hands north of the border. The large horn of a Mexican range saddle gave it the derogatory name applied by Ysabel. Horses carrying only blankets hinted at Indian owners.

As the gates swung closed, Belle saw a tall, handsome officer in the elaborate green uniform of the Austrian Hussars walk up and greet Peraro. She lowered the glasses and looked at her companions.

"I'd say Caillard's called folks in to hear what he's got in mind," Ysabel said, returning his glasses to the pouch.

"It's likely," Belle agreed. "We couldn't have come at a better time. I'll be interested in hearing what he has to say."

"We could ride on over and ask 'em to let us in," the Kid suggested.

"And might get our heads shot off in return," Belle warned. "It's a chance I'd rather not take."

"You got something else in mind, Miss Belle?" asked Rache, his tone showing that he expected the answer to be in the affirmative.

"Not offhand," Belle admitted ruefully.

"Let's go in over the wall," offered the Kid. "I reckon that'd do what you want, Belle."

It had been Belle's intention, if possible, to make a dramatic entrance. One calculated to convince General Caillard that her party would be of greater use to his cause than would Tollinger and Barmain. Having examined the fort, she had doubted if the plan could be carried out.

"It would, Lon," the girl agreed. "But can we do it?"

"Likely, comes dark," the Kid affirmed, patting the forty-foot length of three-strand, hard-plaited Manila rope which hung coiled and strapped to his saddle horn. "We Injun across there, wait until the sentry goes by, toss a loop over the barrel of one of them cannons and climb up."

"It could be done, Belle," Ysabel continued. "You want to, you, me 'n' Lon'll give it a whirl."

"What's up?" demanded Rache belligerently. "Reckon me 'n' Cactus're too old to make it?"

"I know you'd be fool enough to try." Ysabel grinned. "Only, way them sentries keep patroling, there won't be time for more than three of us to get over."

"Hell!" Rache protested and touched his left side. "We've got enough knives to hand them their needings."

"We want to impress Caillard, not rile him by wiping out half of his garrison," Belle reminded the bristling oldster, then smiled in her most winning manner. "Will you play it Sam's way please, boys?"

As if to give another reason for the old-timers staying behind, a mountain lion cut loose with its spine-chilling screech not far away. All the horses moved restlessly. Range-bred, they recognized the danger heralded by the sound. Rache and Cactus realized that they could not leave their mounts unattended with a cougar on the prowl.

"Aw shucks!" Rache replied. "Iffen you wants it that way, Miss Belle, that's how she's going to be."

"We'll lay up back in the woods," Cactus went on. "Then when you want us, we'll drift on over."

Belle felt considerable relief at the old-timers' acceptance. Once inside the fort, she and her escort would be at Caillard's mercy and might not be permitted to leave. So she had sufficient misgivings over endangering the Ysabel family's lives without also dragging the two ancient Texans into peril.

"One thing, though," Rache growled, throwing a disgusted scowl at the Kid's stallion. "You take the saddle off that blasted white snapping turtle yourself. First time he looks like biting me, I'll make wolf bait of him."

"Shucks." The Kid grinned, swinging his horse around. "He won't hurt you none."

"You're danged right he won't," bristled the oldster. " 'Cause I ain't fixing to give him a son-of-a-bitching chance. Being right sorry for saying such words afore you, Miss Belle."

"That's all right, Horatio," Belle commiserated. "He'd make a saint go to cursing. Don't pay him no never mind."

"Danged if they ain't ganging up on me again, *ap'*," groaned the Kid. "I'm going. Saw a clearing by a stream back there a ways that'd make a jim-dandy camping place for us."

Withdrawing from the edge of the *bosque,* they made their way to the Kid's clearing. Once there, no time was wasted on levity. Swiftly they removed the saddles and saw to the horses' needs. Belle's *bayo-cebrunos* and the pack animal had to be hobbled, but the others' mounts could be trusted not to stray and were left free. Then Belle gave thought to her arrival in the fort. She wondered if she should select other clothing from her baggage, but decided against it. Maybe the garments she had in mind would be impressive, but they were not suitable for the manner in which they planned to enter the general's presence. Nor, if it came to a point, were her riding boots.

Mentioning the matter to her companions, she announced her intention of making the climb barefooted. Beaming with pleasure, Rache announced that *he* could solve the girl's problem. Opening his bedroll, he dug into his "thirty-year gatherings"* and produced a pair of calf-high Comanche moccasins. Belle accepted them, tried them on and found that they fitted her snugly.

"Let's get going afore that pesky ole varmint swells up and busts." The Kid grinned, unstrapping his rope and hanging it over his left shoulder. "Bring your glasses, *ap'*, I'd like a closer look over them walls."

The Kid had also donned moccasins and debated the advisability of taking along his Mississippi rifle. Reluctantly he concluded that the rifle's usefulness for displaying accurate

---

* Thirty-year gatherings: personal property, carried in a war bag.

shooting would be outweighed by its awkwardness during the climb. So he left it in its boot.

When everything had been settled, Belle, the Ysabels and Rache returned to the fringe of the *bosque*. Agreeing to stay and watch over the horses, Cactus had given his short companion a dire warning of severe reprisals if Rache attempted to accompany the others all the way.

Keeping concealed, Belle and her escort spent the last minutes of daylight scanning the terrain and examining their objective. Taking his father's field glasses, the Kid climbed a tree and obtained a better view over the walls. On descending, he announced that most of the activity inside the walls seemed to be centering on the large main building. Apart from a few soldiers, the rest of the occupants appeared to be converging on it. Supplementing his early *Pehnane* scout training with experience picked up in the war, he had drawn other, more important conclusions. While the left, right and rear walls each had only one sentry patroling its length, he felt that the front offered the best chance to them. The other sides were too open, with the only steps down from the terreplein placed at the corners.

"We'd have to chance moving along to 'em with the guards on two sides likely to see us," the youngster explained. "The two sentries on the front wall don't have to walk so far, but them gate towers'll keep us hid from the feller on the other side. That jasper on the right never comes by the cannon nearest the gate."

"The front it is, then," Belle said and Ysabel nodded his agreement. "And on the cannon next to the gate."

With the gathering darkness, the soft, melancholy cooing calls of the Coppery-Tailed Trogons among the trees had died away. From the depths of the *bosque* came night noises and a Great Horned Owl gave its eerie cry as it skimmed through the air in search of its prey.

"Let's go," Ysabel ordered, coming to his feet.

Handing the field glasses to Rache, the Kid returned his rope to his shoulder. With a grin at the old-timer, he followed his father and the girl from the shelter of the trees. They advanced cautiously, the girl between the men and watching their every move. Alert for the first hint that the sentries had detected them, their clothing merging into the darkness, taking advantage of every scrap of cover, they approached the front of the fort.

As they drew nearer, and no challenge had been given, they became aware of the noise made by the sentries' feet. Probably there were enclosed casements, although without mounted cannon, beneath the terreplein, acting as stables, stores or accommodation for the lower-ranked members of the garrison. That would account for the dull echoing effect as the sentries marched their beats. The sound would be of help to Belle and her companions.

At last the trio stood in the deeper shadow thrown by the wall and comparatively safe from detection. Looking up, Belle could just make out the barrel of the cannon nearest to the gate as it protruded beyond the embrasure. It would be a small enough target for the Kid's rope, taken with the awkward angle at which he must make his throw.

Shaking out his loop, the Kid stepped back and measured the distance with his eye. He cocked an ear and listened to the footfalls of the sentry on their side of the gate. Satisfied that the man was going away, he took aim, twirled the rope and sent it shooting upward. Missing the barrel, it fell back with a soft, swishing thud. Just as the Kid prepared to throw again, the sentry came to a halt. Instantly the youngster froze and his companions stiffened, straining to discover what had caused the man to stop. Voices drifted to their ears—but conversing in normal tones, not raised in alarm. Apparently the sentry had met his opposite number on the eastern terreplein and paused to have a chat.

At a nod from Ysabel, the Kid tried again. Down fell the rope. Letting out an annoyed hiss, the youngster rebuilt his loop with extra care. A quick whirl and it went upward for the third time—and did not tumble back. With a flick of his wrists, the Kid caused the loop to slide farther along the barrel. Then he drew it tight and tested its security. On the corner of the terreplein, the sentries continued talking, oblivious of the trio behind the walls.

Gripping the rope in both hands, the Kid set his feet against the wall and started to walk upward. Hardly daring to breathe, Belle watched him go higher. Then he disappeared and the rope jerked three times. A glance at Ysabel and Belle took hold to follow the youngster.

Although superbly fit, Belle did not find climbing the wall easy. She forced herself to go on and, after what seemed like an age, saw the square opening of the embrasure just above her.

Suddenly the Kid's arm emerged from the hole and made an urgent downward movement. To her horror, Belle realized that the voices along the wall had ceased and the footsteps resumed.

The sentry was coming back!

There could be no retreating down the rope. If she tried, its movement could betray or she might slip. Either way, the sentry would be alerted and raise the alarm. Setting her teeth grimly, she forced herself to remain still and hung suspended just below the lip of the embrasure.

9

WE'VE ONE MISS BOYD
TOO MANY

After delivering his warning to Belle, the Kid remained crouched behind the big cannon on its *barbette* carriage. His right hand moved swiftly and silently to slide the bowie knife from its sheath. Heavy boots clumping noisily, the sentry came nearer and nearer. The Kid tensed like a great cat waiting to spring. If the sentry kept walking, he would change the pattern of his previous evolutions by passing the cannon. In which case, he could not avoid seeing the Kid—and would likely wind up dead. The trouble with that being the Kid did not think he could silence the soldier without attracting the attention of the men on the east wall.

"Raoul!" called the other sentry, and continued in French, "Come here, quick!"

Turning, just one step before he reached a position where he would suffer the consequences of seeing the Kid, the sentry loped back along the terreplein. A brief conversation reached Belle's and the Kid's ears, although only she could follow its meaning.

"What's wrong?"

"I thought I saw something moving out there!"

Bracing her feet against the hard stone of the wall, Belle gritted her teeth and clenched her hands tighter about the rope. For a few heart-pounding seconds, she wondered if the second sentry had seen her. Then she realized that if he had he would have come to "Raoul" instead of calling for the other to join him. Nor did it seem likely that he had noticed Ysabel, for the big Texan stood flattened against the wall below her.

Which raised the point of who, or what, the soldier had seen.

"I can't see anything!" Raoul declared after a moment.

"Over there!" the second sentry insisted. "Shall I shoot?"

Again Belle's heart seemed to increase its pounding. A shot would bring the remainder of the guard to investigate. Fortunately, Raoul also appreciated the fact.

"You'd better not," he said. "If it's nothing, Sergeant Poncey will have you in the cells."

"Come up!" whispered the Kid, leaning through the embrasure and gripping the girl's left wrist. He had sheathed his knife as soon as the sentry turned away.

With the youngster's help, Belle reached the opening. There was room in plenty alongside the cannon's barrel for her to slip through. Almost before she felt the level surface of the terreplein under her feet, the Kid jerked the rope and signaled to his father to follow.

"Let's go," the Kid hissed. "Pappy'll come's soon's he's up."

"It's still there, I tell you!" the second sentry said. "I saw it move."

Fighting to hold down the sound of her breathing, Belle tiptoed after the Kid across the terreplein and down the stone steps. At the forward eastern corner, the two soldiers continued to debate the possibility of somebody, or something, moving around in the darkness beyond the walls. They were so engrossed that they did not notice the girl and the Kid cross, or, a few seconds later, Ysabel come through the embrasure and follow them.

"What the hell've they se—?" Ysabel began as he joined Belle and the Kid.

As if in answer, they heard a loud, raucous braying sound shatter the silence outside the fort.

"It's only a donkey!" Raoul snorted. "Put down your rifle, you fool. The Austrian pig or Poncey would have the hide flogged off your back if you'd turned out the garrison for that."

"Donkey's right," grinned the Kid, after Belle had interpreted the sentry's comment. "It sure is. Only it's got two legs and a droopy misplaced eyebrow."

"*Rachel!*" Belle gasped.

"Danged ole fool," agreed Ysabel admiringly. "He must've snuck over that ways and moved around just enough for the sentry not to be sure he saw him."

"He certainly helped us," Belle said quietly.

An inner glow of satisfaction filled the girl at this further demonstration of her companions' high regard for her. Without any mention of expecting a reward, making no demands for monetary, material or sexual remuneration for their services, they willingly took desperate chances to help her.

However, one did not stand daydreaming in Belle's current situation. At a sign from Ysabel, they advanced alongside the gate tower. The Kid peered cautiously around the corner and nodded in satisfaction.

"Nobody around," he said.

"Nor any need for us to keep sneaking about now," Ysabel went on.

With that he walked boldly forward. After a moment's hesitation, Belle followed on the Kid's heels. As Ysabel had claimed, there was no further need for them to attempt to avoid being observed. In fact, doing it might easily ruin all they had so far achieved. They would attract less attention if they walked openly than by being caught skulking in the shadows. There were sufficient strangers in the fort for any of its garrison who saw the trio to mistake them for guests.

Going by the noise which rose from it, the large building in the middle of the square must be the center of attraction. It had two stories of solid height, the upper of them apparently being

divided into rooms for offices or officers' living quarters. The
front half of the ground floor was given over to a mess hall.

Before offering to enter the big, closed double doors, Belle
and the Texans paused and looked through one of the windows.
At first-floor level, a gallery overlooked the rear end of the mess
hall. Split into segments, the gallery resembled a row of boxes
at a theater. Half of the segments had drapes drawn across their
fronts.

At that moment, however, Belle felt less interested in the
gallery than with the ground floor. In its center, three long
tables formed an open-ended square. All of the guests had been
seated on the outer sides of the tables so that they received an
uninterrupted view of the men opposite or around them.

"That figures," Ysabel remarked, when his son commented
on the seating arrangements. "I shouldn't reckon any of them
yahoos in there'd trust the others behind their backs."

"No sir," agreed the Kid. "I tell you, that bunch in there
makes even Castro's regular crowd look good."

Damning as the statement might be, Belle felt inclined to
concur with it. Gazing along the two side tables, she failed to
locate Tollinger or Barmain. What she did see was as villain-
ous, cruel and savage a set of faces as had ever come before her
eyes. At the right, she recognized Hoxley's white companion
sitting glowering around and eating. The other guests were
Mexicans, dressed too garishly and well to suit their table manners, Yaquis and a few Indians from more civilized tribes.
Showing none of the impressive dress style of the Plains Indians
from north of the border, the latter sported cast-off Mexican or
white men's clothes and had their hair held back by cloth bands
instead of concealed beneath warbonnets.

Serving the guests were several Mexican and Indian girls.
Each wore a wide-brimmed, low-crowned black hat with a red
plume trailing from it and secured by white ribbons tied in a
bow under the chin. A waist-long blue tunic, in the style worn
by the French infantry, extended to the top of a white apron
hanging over a knee-long, flaring blue skirt encircled by two
white bands. Decorum was preserved by red trousers with a

double blue stripe down the seams. Suspended from the right shoulder on a shining black leather strap, a small wine keg hung at each girl's left hip. Belle recognized the ensemble as the uniform of a *cantinière,* now generally adopted by the French Army.

From the flanks, Belle turned her attention to the center table. There sat the organizers of the plot and the leaders of the various gangs assembled in the hall. Belle identified Hoxley and Peraro, while Sam Ysabel whispered the names of other prominent personages. *Halcón,* Yaqui war chief; Crespo and Yerno, *bandidos* only slightly less prominent than Peraro; Matt Harvey, a British-born ship's captain who combined slave- and blockade-running with piracy along the Mexican coast. Three more Mexicans sat at the top table, but the Ysabels did not know them.

In the center of the gang leaders sat two men and a woman. On the woman's right side, the tall Austrian Hussar colonel watched the guests' table manners with thinly concealed, supercilious disdain.

From what Belle could make out, the woman was a beautiful blonde who would equal her in height. Even seated, she conveyed an impression of possessing a richly endowed, voluptuous figure. The full swell of her bosom showed to its best advantage under a tight scarlet jacket. Gold hussar braiding graced its front and the sleeves bore so-called "Austrian knots" of the same material —resembling the "chicken guts" insignia of the C.S.A. By peering under the table, Belle discovered that the blonde wore matching, skintight breeches with inverted "Austrian knot" patterning. Hessian boots ended just below each knee, with a "V" notch at the front. The martial effect presented by the blonde extended to her having a sword of some kind hanging at her side.

To the left of the woman sat a bear of a man. Big, burly, with a hard, blue-chinned face, he wore the uniform of a French general. In his late forties at least, he had the appearance of a harsh martinet, a driver rather than a leader of men. There could be no doubting his identity. He must be General Gautier

Caillard, commandant of the fort and potential ruler of a separate kingdom.

"Those jaspers you want aren't in there, Belle," commented the Kid.

"No," Belle replied. "They'd be at Caillard's table if they were."

"How about it then?" Ysabel inquired.

"Let's go in," Belle suggested. "And let's make a real entrance."

At the double front doors, Ysabel took the right side and the Kid went to the left. With Belle between them, they turned the handles. On Belle's nod, they pushed hard. Creaking hinges drew attention as the doors swung inward. All around the room conversations died and cold eyes stared suspiciously at the newcomers. Belle strolled in, acting as calm and unconcerned as if she were entering the headquarters of the Confederate Secret Service, with the Ysabels forming barbs to her arrowpoint. In that formation they advanced across the room.

"Up on the balcony, Belle," growled the Kid, hardly moving his lips.

Looking up, Belle saw that some of the gallery's drapes had been drawn open. Soldiers stood lining rifles down at her party, but did not fire. Belle sucked in a breath of exasperation at the sight. Naturally Caillard would take precautions when entertaining that class of visitor. Equally naturally, those precautions would include concealing riflemen on the gallery, from which position they could cover the whole of the mess hall.

Unfortunately, the realization had come too late. In all probability, only the fact that one of the new arrivals was a woman caused the soldiers to hold their fire. One thing was certain. There could be no turning back. So, ignoring the rifles and the cold stares of the men at the tables, the trio kept walking.

An explosive curse broke from Hoxley's lips and he made as if to shove back his chair. Thinking better of it, he remained seated. Belle saw the gesture, but her main interest centered on the trio in the middle of the table. Surprise flickered across Caillard's face, but he made no move. Losing its supercilious expression, the Austrian's handsome features showed mingled bafflement and anger. Looking Belle over from head to toe, the blonde tightened her lips into a grim line. She snapped her fingers and the two *cantinières* attending to the top table moved to her side. Big, buxom, they were of European descent, a red-head and a straw-yellow blonde, good-looking in a large way but with hard mouths.

"I left orders that nobody was to be let in without my authority," the Austrian barked in good English. "Who gave you permission to enter?"

"We didn't ask for it," Belle replied, coming to a halt facing the trio across the table. "We climbed the wall."

"Climbed the—?" the Austrian spat out. "How?"

"Threw a rope over one of the cannon and climbed up," Belle explained.

"That's impossible!" barked the Austrian.

"The rope's still hanging on the cannon," Belle pointed out. "And we're here."

"It seems that your arrangements aren't so perfect after all, Count Otto," Caillard remarked, and Belle thought that she detected a hint of malicious delight at the Austrian being found wanting in his duties.

"Good evening, General Caillard," Belle put in, speaking fluent French. "We heard that you need good fighting men, so we came to offer our services."

"*Your* services?" the blonde challenged coldly.

"My companions and mine," Belle confirmed, then indicated the Texans in turn. "This is Sam Ysabel and his son, *Cabrito*. Or, as we say north of the Rio Grande, the Ysabel Kid."

A brief rumble of talk rose along the flanking tables as the names were repeated. Even the Yaqui chief and the Mexicans from the more southerly districts of the country showed that they had heard of Sam Ysabel and the Kid. Caillard frowned, the Austrian scowled and muttered, while the blonde stared straight at Belle.

"And who are you?" the blonde demanded.

"My name is Belle Boyd," the girl answered. "They call me the Rebel Spy."

While Belle had figured that her name would be known, she hardly expected it to produce such an effect as the trio from the fort displayed. The blonde, Caillard and the Austrian exchanged startled glances, then turned their eyes to Belle in a mixture of mistrust and disbelief. Taking their attention from the Ysabels, Hoxley and Peraro studied the girl with increased interest.

"So you are Belle Boyd, the Rebel Spy?" purred the blonde. "This *is* a surprise. Surely she must join us at our table, Gautier?"

"Of course she must, Sylvie," Caillard replied. "Alice, tell the orderlies to bring chairs for Mademoiselle Boyd and her companions."

"Perhaps the Rebel Spy would like to wash up before she eats?" the blonde suggested. "I will take her to the washroom if she does."

Something in the blonde's tone disturbed Belle. Just what, she could not decide. Maybe Sylvie did not care for the idea of the Rebel Spy being around. If her choice of clothing meant anything, the blonde liked to draw attention her way. Having a beautiful girl, already famous and with solid achievements behind her, in the fort would tend to distract notice from Sylvie. However, there was nothing to be gained by openly antagonizing the blonde. Not, at least, until Belle knew for sure who Sylvie was. A wedding ring and the manner in which she addressed Caillard suggested that she might be his wife.

"Thank you," Belle said. "I would like to wash. Climbing your wall was easy, but it did dirty my hands."

Already the red-haired *cantinière* and two French private soldiers carried chairs from the rear of the room to Caillard's table. Belle and the Ysabels turned, passing through a barrage of interested stares as they walked around the left side table and toward their seats.

Leaving her chair, Sylvie went to meet Belle. Doing so, the blonde displayed her whole figure. Flaunted might be a better word, for her tunic's tight fit set off the mound of her bust, the slenderness of her waist and the curve of her hips; while the breeches emphasized the play of her magnificent thigh and gluteus muscles to the full. An elegant, yet functional, rapier's sheath hung from the slings of her mirror-surfaced black weapon belt. She moved with a sensual attention-drawing grace.

"Come with me, Miss Boyd," Sylvie requested. "I am Madame Caillard."

"I'm pleased to meet you," Belle answered.

"Be seated, gentlemen," Caillard told the Texans, indicating two of the open-backed chairs. "Can I introduce you to any of our other guests?"

"We know most of these gents," Ysabel answered. *"Saludos,* Ramon, Crespo, Yerno, *Halcón.* Howdy there, Matt."

Mutters came back in reply to the greetings and Caillard announced the names of the other three Mexicans; all of whom the Ysabels had heard mentioned but did not know. Then the general indicated the scowling Austrian.

"This is Colonel Count Otto von Bulow."

"Howdy, Colonel," Ysabel drawled, sitting down. "Don't get too riled at your sentries. Me 'n' the boy here, we learned sneaky-moving from Injuns. Whites come easy after that. And Miss Belle steps mighty light on her feet."

Leaving her husband to deal with the Texans, Sylvie escorted Belle under the gallery and toward one of the doors in the wall separating the mess hall from the rear of the ground floor. Both the European *cantinières* followed the blonde and Belle, walking soft-footed as they watched every move the girl made. Opening the door, Sylvie led the way into what appeared to be a smaller dining room. Four more *cantinières,* all Mexicans, were sharing the one table with a fifth woman. Although she was sitting with her back to the door, Belle thought the fifth occupant of the room looked vaguely familiar. As the woman rose and turned, Belle's suspicions became certainties.

Although several years older, the woman equaled Belle's and Sylvie's height. Maybe she lacked their beauty, but she was still good-looking and matched the blonde in the matter of a rich, hourglass figure. Her black hair had been cut as short as Belle's. She wore an open-necked mauve blouse, snug-fitting riding breeches and calf-high boots.

Her name was Eve Coniston and, when she last came into contact with Belle, she had been a member of the United States Secret Service. Which did not explain why she was in Fort Mendez, or the reason for her obvious perturbation at being confronted by the Rebel Spy.

"You seem to know each other," Sylvie purred and, unseen by Belle, the redheaded *cantinière* freed her flask to hold it in both hands.

"We do," Belle agreed. "She is—"

Shoving her chair aside, Eve hurled herself toward Belle. Instantly the girl clenched her fists and prepared to defend herself. Their last meeting had culminated in a fight and, although Belle had just managed to win it, she knew all too well how tough the Yankee could be. Letting out startled and excited exclamations, the four Mexican *cantinières* sprang to their feet.

Before Eve reached Belle, Alice swung up the cask and brought it down on the girl's head. Although Belle's Stetson took the worst of the impact, she still collapsed stunned. Unable to halt her charge, Eve tripped over Belle's body and sprawled forward. Around lashed the blonde *cantinière*'s left fist, thudding against the base of Eve's skull. Plunging helplessly on, Eve collided with the wall and slid limply to the floor. Looking from Belle to Eve, Sylvie snapped orders to the watching women.

Groaning back to consciousness, Belle raised a hand toward her head. Her eyes regained their focus and she became aware that no sleeve covered her arm. As she raised herself into a sitting position and looked down, she discovered that she was naked to the waist and had also lost the borrowed moccasins. Hearing an exclamation, she turned her head in its direction. Clad in nothing but her riding breeches, Eve was being hauled to her feet by two of the Mexican *cantinières*. Hands gripped

Belle by the arms and raised her erect, holding on firmly. Both Belle and Eve struggled, glaring at each other.

"Let me go!" Belle gasped, with Eve repeating the request simultaneously.

"Not yet, little chickens," Alice sneered, standing by the table on which the two girls' removed clothing had been placed. *"Madame la générale* has something better in mind for you." She looked at the blond *cantinière.* "Hasn't she, Marthe?"

At that moment the door behind Belle opened, then closed. Sylvie walked into the girl's view and looked at Eve.

"Who are you?" the blonde demanded.

"Belle Boyd!" Eve replied, in an excellent imitation of a Southern drawl.

"Then who is she?" Sylvie wanted to know, indicating Belle.

"I'm—!" Belle began, only to be silenced by Marthe stepping behind her and reaching forward to clap a hand over her mouth.

"She used to work for me in the war," Eve explained.

"Is that true?" Sylvie asked, turning toward Belle.

Meeting Eve's eyes as the hand left her mouth, Belle thought fast. At that moment she held Eve's life in her hands just as surely as Eve had held Belle's when they had been captured by Mexican *bandidos.* Then Eve had held her tongue, saving Belle from torture, if not death. So Belle knew that she could not denounce Eve as a Yankee spy.

"In reverse," Belle replied. "I'm Belle Boyd. She was the madam of a whorehouse who used to get information for me."

"It seems we've one Miss Boyd too many," Sylvie said and her eyes glinted maliciously. "Fortunately, the solution is not difficult. We have all heard of how tough the Rebel Spy is; and I had promised my husband that I would provide entertainment for our—guests." Her lips twisted derisively as she uttered the last word. "You have presented me with a way of doing it and of solving the problem of your identity."

"How?" Belle asked, although she and Eve could guess.

"You will be taken into the mess hall," Sylvie informed them.

"There you will be released and one of you must make the other confess that she is a liar."

"And if we refuse?" asked Eve.

"I'll have you both handed over to the—guests," Sylvie replied. "On the other hand, the Rebel Spy will be made welcome and the liar will be given to our guests for their pleasure. Take them around and bring them in through the main entrance, *cantinières*. If they make trouble for you, cripple them. I doubt if the men we are entertaining will care if they can't walk."

10
I WISH TO SAVE YOUR LIVES

Although the Kid and his father had noticed Sylvie come from the room into which she had taken Belle, they felt no concern. The blonde had crossed to the table and whispered in her husband's ear, then spoken with the orderlies. Nothing suspicious had happened and she retired from the hall. Plates loaded with thick steaks, potatoes and beans were placed before the Texans. Around the room, talk continued while knives, forks or fingers transferred food to mouths. Neither of the Texans paid any great attention to the orderlies hovering in the background, but waited for Belle to return.

Not until the main doors opened and Sylvie walked in did Ysabel and the Kid begin to wonder why Belle had not rejoined them. Advancing to the center of the open space before the tables, Sylvie halted and raised her hands. What that did to her garments brought silence to the supper guests quicker than the gesture's meaning alone would have. Watching the blonde, the Ysabels failed to observe the orderlies drawing Lefaucheux revolvers and moving cautiously toward them.

"Senors!" Sylvie called and pointed toward the doors. "For your entertainment—"

Anything more she might have planned to say was drowned by the rumble of excited comment that arose as the *cantinières* hustled Belle and Eve into the room. Immediately, before the Kid and his father could do more than start to push back their chairs, the orderlies obeyed orders. The Kid felt the hard muzzle of a revolver ram into his back, but still tensed to continue rising.

"Sit still, gentlemen!" Caillard ordered, leaning forward to look at the Texans.

"Do it, Lon!" Ysabel growled, guessing that his son also had a gun boring against his spine.

For all his anger, the Kid could still think. He knew that to resist would not only be futile, but fatal. With an effort, he controlled his impulse to rise. Sinking back onto his chair, he sat without movement. At that moment, he looked every inch a Comanche. Not just an ordinary member of the *Nemenuh,* but a *Pehnane* Dog Soldier ready to go on the rampage. Looking sideways, Ysabel knew his son was sitting at hair-trigger readiness. The big Texan hoped that the Kid would not do anything foolish or rash.

"I wish to save your lives, gentlemen," Caillard announced, still facing the Ysabels. "If you tried to interfere, my other guests would kill you."

"These two women both claim to be the Rebel Spy," Sylvie announced. "So they will fight to see who tells the truth. The loser is for you."

Savage curses in the slow-tongued *Pehnane* dialect blasted from the Kid's lips, to be swamped under by the raucous, ebullient comments bouncing among the other guests. With the exception of the Ysabels—and possibly Caillard and von Bulow —every man in the room studied Belle and Eve from two separate angles. First, as contestants in a fight on which money could be bet. Second, in the light of what could be done to the loser. Certainly they all figured that the next few minutes might prove to be sensationally entertaining, with the added attraction of venting their aroused sexual stimulations on one or the other of the white women.

Sufficiently good-looking under normal conditions to interest men, Eve had aged well. Exposed to view and unsupported, the twin hemispheres of her breasts thrust out pink-tipped and firm, sagging only slightly despite their size. Her waist slimmed without artificial aids, while her stomach was flat and gave a hint of its muscular hardness. Weight would favor her and she probably had the advantage of strength, for her biceps showed good development, although not to the point of being un-feminine.

By comparison with Eve, Belle's small-busted, slim-hipped frame seemed almost boyish. Yet her high, slightly uptilted breasts and beautiful features dispelled such notions as soon as they came. There stood a gorgeous woman, even in an age when a more buxom figure was considered the acme of female pulchritude. Taken in collation with Eve, for the forthcoming fight, the men noted the muscular effect of Belle's legs within the skintight breeches and the steel-spring firmness of her arms and body. Both told of speed and power. Maybe she was lighter, but the Ysabel family's companion might be a match for the other woman.

Reconciled to the fact that a fight could not be avoided, Belle and Eve allowed the *cantinières* to guide them into the open space between the tables. To resist would be useless and merely drain away energy that might make all the difference between victory and defeat later on. Both of them burned with humiliation and embarrassment as they were turned, still securely held, to face each other. On three sides, lascivious eyes and drooling mouths turned their way. They could guess at the thoughts running through the male onlookers' heads, but fought to quell their revulsion and concentrate on what lay ahead.

Thinking back to the savage brawl on the banks of the Rio Grande, Eve tried to decide which tactics would offer her the best chance of winning. The *cantinières* had removed her rings and her fingernails were too short to make effective weapons. While they had also taken her shoes, the same applied to Belle, for which Eve felt thankful. Even barefooted, the slim Rebel girl's *savate* training could be put to use, but not so effectively.

Mingled with the revulsion she felt, Belle experienced a thrill of anticipation. Despite the publicity accorded to the so-called "Scout of the Cumberland," Pauline Cushman,* Eve Coniston had been the Union's best and most capable female spy. Belle had always been proud of her professional ability, including her skill in the art of self-defense, and last time she had been brought very close to defeat at Eve's hands. Only the Ysabel family's explosive destruction of the bribe money had given Belle the respite she desperately needed by distracting Eve. Often in the past months, Belle had wondered if she could have beaten Eve without it. So she found herself waiting almost eagerly to try conclusions against the Yankee agent once more, this time without interruptions or distractions. Meeting Eve's gaze, Belle realized that much the same conjecture and eagerness ate at her.

While the *cantinières* led Belle and Eve into position, Sylvie had backed out of the combat area.

"Now!" the blonde snapped in Spanish.

Instantly the women holding the contestants' arms propelled them at each other, releasing them and hurrying away to join Sylvie. An anticipatory hush dropped on the room as the onlookers realized that the spectacle was about to commence.

Although Belle had hoped that they would be turned loose and allowed to make their own way at each other, the *cantinières'* actions did not permit it. Instead, she and Eve rushed together on a collision course. Bare feet slapping on the hard-packed earth floor, unable to stop herself, Belle threw a punch with her right fist. At the same moment, Eve's left hand lashed in Belle's direction. Even as the girl's bony knuckles rammed into Eve's mouth, she felt the woman's fist impact on the side of her cheek. The blows stung, but did no real damage; then Belle and Eve came together.

Drawing closer, they continued to use their fists. Belle bored in, her hard fists bombarding Eve's bust and midsection. Oblivi-

* Some of Pauline Cushman's story is told in "The Major" episode of *The Texan*.

ous of the pain, Eve hooked powerful punches into the girl's stomach, ribs and breasts. In the space of ten seconds at least a dozen blows landed on each of them, ending any remaining compunctions the recipients might have felt about fighting.

Instinct and a desire to escape from the punishing fists caused them to move nearer to each other. Up rammed Belle's left knee, but Eve had either expected it or was lucky. Twisting to the right, she took the attack on her thigh and threw her left arm around behind Belle's neck. Belle's right arm hooked around Eve's torso, linking hands with her left as it passed down over the woman's shoulder. Locked together in that way, they wrestled with spread-apart legs, each trying to throw the other from her feet.

More by luck than intention, Eve hooked her right leg behind Belle's left knee. Still locked breast to breast, they lost their footing and went to the floor. Belle landed on the bottom, with Eve kneeling astride her and driving a punch into her ribs. Heaving upward, Belle tipped the woman over only to be turned. As she assumed the lower position again, she locked her legs about Eve's waist. Crossing her ankles, Belle strived for crushing pressure and to prevent Eve drawing far enough away to ram those short jabs into her. Riding and other strenuous exercise had given Belle exceptionally strong leg muscles, so the compression they applied to Eve's kidney region was painful in the extreme. Gasping, spitting incoherent threats, Eve tried to free herself. With Belle's arms enfolding her neck, she could not bring her fists into play.

Twice they rolled over, without any slackening of Belle's holds. Then Eve's face pressed against Belle's left shoulder, mouth opening to close on flesh. A screech broke from Belle's lips as the burning sharpness of the bite stabbed into her. Feeling the girl's arms and legs loosen, Eve placed her hands on the floor and forced upward. Her torso came free from Belle's arms, but the legs tightened again before she could escape. Flashing across, Belle's left fist caught Eve's nose and blood splashed down onto the girl. Eve's hands flailed in return, slapping Belle's face and rocking her head from side to side. When that failed, Eve stabbed her fingers toward the girl's bust. Just in time Belle caught the woman's wrists and held the clutching hands away from the ultrasensitive region.

Struggling to her knees, shaking and pulling to free her wrists, Eve managed to regain her feet. Still Belle clung to the scissors hold, dangling in front of her victim with the tenacity of a bulldog nailing onto a beef-critter's nose. Releasing Eve's wrists, Belle spread her arms on the floor to prevent herself being rolled over and attempted to tilt the other off balance. Digging her fingers into the tops of Belle's thighs, Eve also rammed her knees into the girl's back, but was too close to put any force behind them. So Eve balanced herself on her right leg, curling the left around the girl's slender middle. Just too late Belle saw the danger. Thrusting downward, Eve raked the heel of her foot over the bottom of the girl's right breast. Gasping, Belle opened her legs. The stamp had hurt but not incapacitated her. Swinging her feet from behind Eve, she propelled them into the woman's belly. If Belle could have put her full strength behind the kick, the fight would have been as good as over. As it was, Eve reeled back a few steps before catching her balance and halting.

Yells of encouragement rose from the onlookers as Eve's body literally soared through the air in her eagerness to get at Belle. The woman landed flush on Belle with a loud smack reminiscent of a side of beef being flung onto a table. Momentarily, the impact knocked the breath from both of them. Then, as Eve's hands dug into Belle's short hair, the girl hooked her right hand under and between the woman's spread-apart, kneeling legs and heaved her over. Rolling on top, Belle felt Eve's legs close about her. Feeling Belle rear back, Eve raised her rump from the floor and used her legs to throw the girl from her. They started to rise, then flung themselves at each other before reaching higher than their knees.

Squirming, contorting and twisting, the two women thrashed over and over on the floor. Gasps, squeals, harsh screeches broke from them, mingling with the constant barrage of excited comment and suggestions rising on all sides. In addition to the impact of flat palms, knuckles, elbows, knees, feet and foreheads against whatever part of the opponent's body happened to be most readily available, their teeth came into play. However, their short hair, especially when it became slick with sweat, offered a poor gripping surface. On more than one occasion, clutching fingers slipped from their hold and threw their user off balance. When that happened, a surging heave would see the recipient of the abortive hair-pull momentarily in ascendancy.

For five minutes with barely a pause, the wild, savage, rolling mill continued. Excited men stood on their chairs or climbed onto the tables to obtain a better view. Bets were still being made, on which girl would win, how long the fight would last or even who would gain the next brief advantage. Faces twisted with lust as the sexual stimulation, caused by watching the half-naked bodies twirling and gyrating, grew among the male members of the audience.

"Can't we stop it, *ap*?" growled the Kid, his respect for Belle causing a revulsion that prevented him from sharing the other men's emotions.

Even as he spoke, the Kid became aware that the revolver was no longer boring into his back. Instead, the orderly who had been covering him now stood at his side. The Lefaucheux hung with its barrel pointing at the floor, while the soldier stared with rapt attention at Eve and Belle. Reaching out, the Kid gripped the gun. Such was the orderly's fascination in the fight that he did no more than glare furiously at the Kid for a moment before relinquishing the weapon and returning his gaze to the women.

"Not yet, boy!" Ysabel warned as he saw his son tense. "We'd have to fight the whole blasted boiling of 'em if we tried to stop it. And likely get Belle killed along of us."

Bitterly, the Kid relaxed. He knew that his father had called the play correctly. So, no matter how much doing it went against the grain, they must allow the fight to go on to the end. One thing the Kid swore to himself, whether Belle won or lost, nobody in the crowd would lay hands on either woman if he could prevent it. Glancing sideways, the Kid saw that the second orderly was also neglecting his duty. Leaning across the table to improve his view, he had actually laid down his revolver. Going by the rapt manner in which Caillard and von Bulow were following the brawl, they had not noticed the soldiers' abandonment of duty.

Returning his attention to the space between the tables, the Kid saw that Belle and Eve had managed to rise. Still clinging together, they spun around three times. Relinquishing her hold, Belle rained a battery of punches into Eve's body. Gasps of almost breathless pain whistled through Eve's lips. Desperate to halt the impact of the bony knuckles against her stomach and bust, she threw her right arm around Belle's neck and twisted to the left until she was standing alongside the girl. With a ripping sound, Eve's breeches split down the rear seam as she slammed her right thigh against the back of Belle's left knee and heaved on the girl's right shoulder.

Thrown off balance, Belle fell with enough force to roll her along the floor. Running after her, Eve stamped hard on her side. Croaking with pain, Belle tried to crawl away. Eve swooped down, caught Belle by the hair and the left arm to drag her erect. Another rapid exchange of blows followed before pain goaded Eve to repeat the throw. Again Eve followed Belle, the waistband keeping her breeches up with the aid of the material clinging to her sweat-sodden skin. The older woman showed signs of the exhaustion that welled through her pain-filled body as she halted and raised her foot. Bringing it down, she tottered slightly on her supporting leg. She felt her heel strike, but slide from Belle's perspiration-saturated shoulder and finished up standing astride the girl facing Belle's feet.

Sobbing for breath, Belle sat up. She interlaced her fingers and slammed her linked hands behind Eve's rump. Knocked forward by the attack, Eve stumbled and only remained upright with an effort. By the time she had stopped and turned, Belle had already regained her feet and was advancing. With fingers crooked like talons, Eve lunged to meet the girl. Stepping aside at the last moment, Belle inclined her torso to the left. Drawing up her right leg, she swung it in a *savate* horizontal side kick. Continuing to move forward, Eve took the top of Belle's instep in the stomach. Breath burst from Eve's tormented lungs and she gripped at the nearest table to prevent herself from falling.

Moaning a little, Eve managed to turn toward Belle. By spreading her feet apart, Eve contrived to keep her balance. Weakly she raised her hands in an attempt to ward off her younger assailant. Gathering her flagging reserves of energy, Belle leapt into the air. Pointing her toes downward, she bent her legs and her knees rammed with sickening force into the bottoms of Eve's breasts. A shriek of agony burst from the woman and she spun away from Belle. Hands clutching at the stricken area, she dropped to her knees by the end of the left side table.

Belle thought that the fight was over. Landing from the leaping double-knee high kick, she clutched at the left-hand table for support. With a feeling of horror, she watched Eve dragging herself erect with its aid. Pure guts alone raised the woman upright. She stood with her shoulders slumped in exhaustion, face contorted with suffering and legs buckling like candles left standing close to a fire. Weakly Eve pawed in Belle's direction, trying to hold off the inevitable. Catching Eve's left wrist in both hands, Belle carried it upward. Pivoting under the trapped arm, she twisted it in a hammerlock behind Eve's back. Then Belle stamped her right foot behind Eve's right knee. Forcing Eve down, Belle thrust the woman's left breast against the corner of the table. Although rounded instead of coming to a point, the corner ground into Eve's already bruised, throbbing breast with savage, numbing, sickening pressure.

"Tell them who I am!" Belle demanded, relaxing her grip slightly.

At first Eve made no reply, other than moaning piteously. Once more Belle forced her against the hard, unyielding wood. A scream of torment burst from Eve and Belle repeated the words.

"Sh-She—B-Boyd!" Eve babbled almost hysterically, her body contorting weakly in pain.

With a swinging heave, Belle dragged Eve from the table and released her. Going down, the Yankee spy turned and lay with arms thrown out wide and legs moving spasmodically. All but overcome by nausea and exhaustion, Belle hobbled across the floor toward the other woman. The girl halted spraddle-legged above the nearly motionless figure. Bending, she sank her fingers into Eve's raw-looking left breast. Blood ran from its nipple tract as Belle dragged Eve upward. Through the swirling mists that seemed to fill her head, Belle saw that Eve's head lolled back, mouth open and working soundlessly, eyes glassy and unseeing. Slowly the exhausted girl released the breast and Eve's torso slumped back limply to the floor.

Seeing that the fight had ended, an Indian standing on the upper end of the right-side table let out a wild whoop. Bounding to the floor on the inside, he ran toward where Belle was standing over the unconscious Eve.

Catapulting to his feet, the Kid sent his chair flying behind him. Out came his bowie knife and his right arm swung upward. Driving down savagely it propelled the knife through the air. Catching the Indian between the shoulders, the point of the blade spiked home. Throwing up his arms, he blundered by the women and tumbled facedown beyond them.

From hurling the knife, the Kid's hand dipped, turned palm out and plucked the big Dragoon Colt from its holster. Still completing his draw, he slapped the left palm onto the table's top and vaulted across. As he landed, he saw a Mexican to the left dropping to the floor and reaching for a gun. Swiveling around, the Kid lined the Dragoon and squeezed its trigger. Black powder swirled as the old revolver roared. Catching the *bandido* in the chest, the .44 ball flung him backward. Ignoring the sight of his second victim striking the table, then collapsing, the Kid sprinted to Belle's side.

Almost as quick off the mark as his son, Ysabel rose the moment it became obvious the fight had ended. Catching the orderly by the shoulder, the big Texan swung him from the table and sent him spinning across the room. Then Ysabel snatched up the man's Lefaucheux and bounded by the chairs of *Halcón* and Yerno to reach Caillard's side.

"Tell 'em to keep back!" Ysabel commanded, ramming the French revolver's barrel into the general's ribs. "You're dead if you don't!"

For a moment Caillard just sat and stared, still drooling in the erotic stimulus created by watching the fight. The crash of the Dragoon jolted him back to reality and an understanding of his position. Already more of the less important guests showed signs of going forward to collect what they regarded as their legitimate spoils. If that happened, Caillard knew the big Texan would carry out his threat. A man of Ysabel's kind did not lightly make such minatory statements.

"Gentlemen!" Caillard yelled. "Stand away. Tell your men to keep off!"

Realizing that the words had been directed at them, the gang leaders put aside any aspirations they might have harbored toward Eve. However, all knew that halting the inflamed passions of their men might take some doing. Feeling Ysabel's acquired revolver gouge harder against his ribs, Caillard took a firmer line of action.

"Guards!" the general roared, turning in his chair to look up at the gallery. "Shoot down any man, other than the American, who tries to go near the women."

Discipline ingrained by long, hard years of service drove the riflemen to make ready to obey. More than that, they felt admiration and a wish to prevent abuses to the women who had fought so gamely, especially as they would be unable to share in the benefits of Eve's defeat. Seeing the rifles lining downward, the men around the tables were not so excited that they would risk going against Caillard's commands.

Nor were the riflemen the only factor to make the guests change their minds. Halting by Belle as she sank to her hands and knees over Eve, the Kid swung slowly around. There was something in his appearance that screamed warnings to the experienced *bandidos* and Yankee hard cases. Even Harvey's British contingent knew that the menacing young figure in the black clothing spelled sudden, unhesitating death to anybody foolish enough to cross him. To the Indians, the signs stood out with complete clarity. No matter how he might be dressed, there stood one of their own race, a name warrior who had counted coup twice already and was prepared to add to his score.

"Young man!" Sylvie said loudly in the lull that followed her husband's threat. "We accept that your friend is the Rebel Spy. No harm will come to her, but the other one pays the penalty."

Although the words seemed to come from very far away, Belle heard and understood them. Slowly she raised her head, shook it and looked around. Despite all Eve had done to her in the course of the savage brawl, Belle could not bear the thought of the loser's penalty being inflicted on the woman.

"N—No—!" Belle croaked, then her pain-drugged mind worked and produced a possible way of saving Eve. "I—I—want—her—my—ser-servant."

"Never!" Sylvie shouted as the Kid translated Belle's request into Spanish. "I said the guests could have the loser."

Stepping away from Belle, the Kid bent and plucked his knife from the Indian's back. Then he returned to the girl's side. Holding the bowie knife, with its gory blade, in his left hand and the cocked Dragoon revolver in the right, he once more swung around.

"All right," the Kid said. "Whoever wants her can have her. All they have to do is get by me!"

For a few seconds the silence hung heavy and charged with menace. Completely spent by her exertions, Belle subsided limply onto Eve and they both lay without a movement.

"By God, Texas!" Hoxley suddenly bellowed, standing up. "I'm with you!"

"And me!" Harvey went on, also rising. "Nobody'll touch that woman if I've anything to do about it."

Instantly Caillard recognized the danger. With the Anglo-Saxons banding together, the Mexicans and Indians might also combine. If so, his meeting could dissolve in smoke, burning powder and roaring guns. That must be prevented at all costs.

"Come, gentlemen," Caillard boomed, trying to sound more jovial than he felt. "We've seen a good fight. Now let us drink to the two gallant ladies' health and leave them be."

"Cantinières!" von Bulow went on, ignoring the furious expression twisting at Sylvie's face. "Pour wine for all."

"That's a whole heap better," drawled Ysabel as the *cantinières* moved to carry out the order. Laying the Lefaucheux on the table, he continued. "Now I want Belle and the other gal getting out of here and their hurts tended to."

"Of course," Caillard answered. "Miss B—the other woman has been given a room upstairs. Who is she, by the way?"

"I dunno," Ysabel lied, for he had recognized Eve but wanted to wait until he had talked with Belle before denouncing the Yankee spy. "Best ask her, or Miss Boyd in the morning."

"I will," Caillard promised, watching the guests resume their seats and accept the wine. Raising his voice, he ordered the two European *cantinières* to take Belle and Eve upstairs and see that the fort's surgeon treated their injuries. He turned to Ysabel and went on. "Take your seat, sir."

"I'll be down again after I've seen Miss Belle's all right," Ysabel answered and walked around the tables to join the Kid.

11
I WANT THE LIVES OF TWO
OF YOUR MEN

Groaning a little, Belle Boyd swung her feet from the bed in the small room to which she and Eve had been carried the previous night. Daylight streamed in at its window and going by the sun's position, she guessed the time to be midmorning. Every muscle of her naked body seemed stiff and protested at being used, while numerous bruises and a few bites sent stabs of pain through her. Her top lip and nose felt as if they were swollen to twice their normal size. Looking down, she studied the discolored patches caused by Eve's attacks or contact with the floor. A shudder ran through the girl. That had been one hell of a fight and she hoped that she might never have to go through another like it.

With that in mind, Belle looked across the room. Vaguely she seemed to remember that Eve had been brought upstairs with her. Everything after Belle's collapse had been hazy. She recalled that the *cantinières* had bathed her and Eve, then the fort's surgeon had attended to their injuries. After that, Belle had been put into the reasonably comfortable bed and Eve laid on a mattress in the corner of the room.

Forcing herself to rise, Belle crossed and looked down at

Eve. Drawing aside the blanket, Belle saw that Eve's naked body carried a mottling of bruising in excess to her own. The swollen, inflamed breasts rose and fell so steadily that Belle felt sure Eve must be under heavy sedation. She would be in too great pain to sleep with such evident ease and soundness.

Hearing the door open, Belle covered Eve and turned indignantly. Marthe and one of the Mexican *cantinières* entered, carrying Belle's packsaddle trunks. Admiration and not a little awe showed on the women's faces as they found the girl on her feet.

"Your men have brought your baggage, *mademoiselle*," Marthe announced in French. "And General Caillard says that we are to attend you."

"Thank you," Belle answered in the same language. "I would like a bath, a meal and to dress. Then I would like an interview with the general if he can spare the time to see me."

"That one still sleeps, I see," Marthe commented, setting her burden on the bed. "The surgeon gave her laudanum to ease the pain."

"I bet she needed it," the Mexican girl put in. Clearly she understood sufficient French to follow the conversation. "You beat her good, *senorita.*"

"*Madame la générale* has a *douche*-bathe in her quarters, *mademoiselle*," Marthe said, glaring her companion to silence. "She's gone riding with the Austrian. You can use it before she comes back."

Something in the way Marthe spoke of Sylvie Caillard hinted to Belle that the blonde might be unpopular with the *cantinières*. If Marthe had been alone in her dislike, she would never have used the mocking name *"madame la générale"* with the Mexican girl present. It was a point worth remembering, for Belle felt sure that Sylvie would be an implacable enemy.

"*Cabrito* and the little old one are outside, *senorita*," the Mexican said. "They ask if you are all right."

"Tell them I'm fine," Belle replied and wished that she was speaking the truth.

Opening one of her trunks, Belle produced a robe. By the time she had put it on, the message had been delivered and the passage cleared for her to go unobserved to Sylvie's room. Accompanied there by Marthe, Belle took pleasure in using *madame la générale*'s private shower bath, knowing that Sylvie would be furious if she learned of it. The cold water refreshed Belle and, for a time at least, soothed away the aches in her body. On returning to her room, she found Eve was still unconscious. Although Belle had hoped to learn what had brought the woman to Fort Mendez, posing as herself, before meeting Caillard, she knew that would be impossible. So she made her preparations for the forthcoming interview.

From her second trunk she took the cadet-gray uniform of a Confederate States cavalry colonel. She had been awarded the rank for her services to the South and to invest her with authority when dealing with military personnel. Slipping into clean underclothes and a blouse, she put on socks and the tight-legged, yellow-striped breeches, then drew shining Hessian boots into place. Wincing a little, she donned her tunic. Copied from a style made popular by a Lieutenant Mark Counter*— with whom she and the Kid would become well acquainted in the future†—it did not blindly conform with the *Manual of Dress* regulations. Double-breasted, it had the formal two rows of seven buttons on its front, the triple one-eighth-of-an-inch gold braid "chicken guts" insignia of a field officer on the sleeves, and three five-pointed gold stars, denoting a full colonel, graced its stand-up collar. However, the skirt "extending halfway between hip and knee" had not been included. Instead of wearing a black silk cravat, she knotted a tight-rolled green scarf of the same material about her throat and let its ends dangle free.

An official weapon belt came next, being buckled about her waist just a touch loosely to avoid pressure on her bruised sides.

* Mark Counter's history is told in the author's floating outfit stories.
† The Kid's first meeting with Mark is in *The Ysabel Kid* and Belle's is in *The Bad Bunch*.

From the bottom of her trunk, she lifted a magnificent rapier. Specially built to suit her, it rode in a sheath designed to be carried on the slings of her belt. At the sight of the sword, Marthe gave a low exclamation. The sound confirmed Belle's suspicions that Sylvie would not approve of her dressing in uniform and wearing a weapon. That only hardened Belle's resolve, for she meant her appearance to be an open challenge to the blonde.

The trunk next yielded a correctly made officer's peaked forage cap. Although that particular style of headgear had never been noted for beauty, Belle gave it an air of style and attractiveness as she perched it jauntily on her head.

Having been to the kitchen while Belle was bathing, the Mexican *cantinière* returned bearing a large, loaded tray. Belle started to make a good breakfast and Alice, the second of the French *cantinières,* arrived to say that General Caillard wished to interview her as soon as convenient. Alice almost duplicated Marthe's reaction on discovering how Belle was attired.

"Tell the general, with my compliments, that I'll join him in half an hour," Belle requested. "And ask my companions if they will meet me here, please."

"Oui, mademoiselle," Alice answered and left the room.

By the time Belle had eaten her breakfast, Marthe appeared to say that the Ysabel family, Rache and Cactus had arrived. After the *cantinières* had left with the tray, Belle collected a pad of the forged fifty-dollar bills from her trunk and slipped it into her tunic's breast pocket. Giving the motionless Eve a glance, the girl left her room. The waiting men grinned appreciatively as they saw the way she was dressed, for she made an attractive picture.

"I'm all right, I assure you," Belle replied in answer to her escort's inquiries about her health. "Rache, will you and Cactus stay on guard here, please?"

"Sure will, Miss Belle," Rache agreed without hesitation and Cactus nodded his assent. "Reckon the Frogs'll try to rob you?"

"I doubt it, although they might want to search my baggage," the girl answered. "It's the woman I fought—"

"If she comes round making fuss—!" Rache bristled.

"Way she looked after the fight," the Kid said, grinning, "I'd say that's not *real* likely."

"She's in there," Belle went on, indicating the door. "I don't want her harming, or *questioning*. You can let the post surgeon see her, but nobody else."

"We'll see to it," promised Cactus. "What if she wants to leave?"

"As Lon would say, that's not real likely. But if she tries, tell her that I want her to stay until I can talk to her."

"She'll be here when you want her," Rache promised.

Leaving the two old-timers sitting outside her door, Belle accompanied the Kid and his father. Due to her condition the previous night, Belle had seen nothing of her surroundings. So she let the Ysabels guide her along the passage and down a flight of stairs to a small hall lined with doors. On the way, she learned what had happened after she was carried from the mess hall.

"Wasn't much," Ysabel told her. "Caillard spouted some about taking over down this ways, and how them's helped him'd do right well out of it. Then he set to getting 'em all drunk and it got sort of forgot about."

"What's that Yan—" the Kid began.

"Her name's Eve—Caterham," Belle interrupted quickly. "She ran a hog ranch—I think you Texans call it—and used to pick up information for Cousin Rose and me."

"Why's she here?" the Kid insisted.

"We haven't discussed it," Belle admitted with a wry smile.

At which point the Texans became aware of how stiffly she was walking and noticed that her face showed occasional hints of the pain she must still feel.

"You sure you're all right, Miss Belle?" Ysabel asked worriedly.

"I was until you started to say 'Miss' again," she replied, then nodded to where a French sergeant major was coming from the door which bore Caillard's name. "That's where we're going."

Showing his surprise at the sight of Belle's uniform, the sergeant major listened to her request that she and the Ysabels be admitted to the general's presence. Returning to the room he had just left, he emerged after a moment and told them to go in. The Kid and his father saw the girl set her face into a stolid mask, square her shoulders and march by the warrant officer. Following, they found Caillard seated at his desk, with von Bulow standing to his right. Across the room, Sylvie turned from the window. A low hiss broke from the blonde's lips as she stared at Belle, then glanced down at her own uniform. Without as much as a flicker of her eyes in Sylvie's direction, Belle marched smartly to the desk. Coming to a halt, the girl threw Caillard a brisk salute that cost her plenty in sharp twinges of protest from stiff, sore muscles.

"Miss Boyd—" Caillard started to say, returning her salute before he could stop himself.

"Colonel Boyd of the Confederate States Army's Secret Service, General," Belle corrected and took a sheet of paper from the pouch on the left of her belt. "My credentials, sir."

Accepting and examining the paper, Caillard found it to be a document identifying Belle. It also gave a description of her, along with the information that she held the rank of colonel with seniority from January the first, 1862. It was signed by General Robert E. Lee.

"My pleasure, Colonel Boyd," Caillard said, rising and returning the paper. "You are over your exertions, I hope?"

"I am, sir," the girl answered.

"Will you have a chair, Colonel?" von Bulow offered, fetching one and ignoring Sylvie's disapproving sniff at the repeated use of Belle's rank.

"Thank you," Belle answered, throwing a dazzling smile at the Austrian and noticing that it drew a glare of hatred from the blonde.

As Belle sat down, the Ysabels ranged themselves on either side of her and stood with thumbs hooked into their gun belts.

"May I ask why you came here, Colonel Boyd?" Caillard said and Belle sensed that he used the word to increase his wife's antipathy toward her.

"As I told you last night," Belle replied, "we, Sam Ysabel, *Cabrito,* the other two Texans and I, have heard what you plan to do. So we came to offer our services. I think that you will find they are worth accepting."

"In what way?" Sylvie demanded, stalking across the room to sit on the edge of the desk between Belle and von Bulow.

"I think I proved my identity last night," Belle said, touching her discolored left cheek with a fingertip. "But if there are still doubts, I will answer them with bare hands, a revolver or a sword." She paused, looking straight at Sylvie. For a moment their eyes locked, then the blonde swung her head away. Smiling, Belle went on, "You will have my services as a spy, General; or in any other active capacity you require. In addition, the Ysabels, Rache and Cactus will join you. I think last night they gave you convincing proof of their worth."

Although Belle could only vaguely remember the Kid's intervention, the fact that Eve Coniston was still alive and unmolested told her that pressure had been brought on Caillard to rescind his wife's stipulations about the fight.

Caillard let out a grunt that might have expressed agreement. When Belle had thrown the challenge at his wife, he had sat back as if expecting her to accept it. Going by his scowl, he had been disappointed by Sylvie's lack of response.

"Besides that, General," Belle continued, "I can offer an even greater contribution to your cause."

"What might that be?" Sylvie hissed.

"Money," Belle answered, taking out the wad of forged bills and tossing them onto the desk's top before Caillard. "Or what will pass for it."

Interest, and not a little greed, flickered across the general's face as he took up and thumbed over the sheaf of what looked like genuine fifty-dollar bills. However, Sylvie let out a depreciating snort.

"That's not much," the blonde said.

"They're forgeries," Belle explained. *"Undetectable* forgeries. I can put into your hands, General, the plates, inks and sufficient paper to print between five hundred and seven hundred and fifty thousand dollars. One could buy a lot of arms and ammunition with them."

"You have them with you?" Caillard breathed.

"You didn't expect me to say 'yes,' General," Belle flattered. "I can have them brought here, after we have come to terms."

"Terms?" Sylvie repeated.

"We're not doing this for charity," Belle pointed out. "Tell the general what you want, Sam."

"A big *hacienda,"* Ysabel drawled. "And the right to run anything I want over the Rio Grande without the revenuers bothering me. That'll do me 'n' the boy. Rache 'n' Cactus'll settle for top fighting wages and a share of any loot that's going."

"And what is your price, Colonel Boyd?" von Bulow inquired.

"I want the lives of two of your men," Belle announced quietly.

Coming to her feet, Sylvie stared at the girl. Caillard and von Bulow stiffened and gave Belle even greater attention. There was no doubt about her sincerity.

Sucking in a deep breath, Caillard asked, "Which two, M— Colonel Boyd?"

"I know them as Tollinger and Barmain."

So did the Caillards and von Bulow, going by their expressions. In fact, learning the identities of her proposed victims appeared to have handed the trio a greater shock than had hearing the price of Belle's enlistment to their cause. Sylvie seemed to be on the point of delivering a vehement refusal. Looking at her, von Bulow gave a slight, but definite, shake of his head. With a thinly veiled show of reluctance, the blonde kept her mouth closed. Belle had seen the byplay and wondered what lay behind it.

"They aren't here at the moment," Caillard claimed. "Would I be permitted to ask why you want to kill them?"

"They murdered my parents," Belle replied.

"I see," the general grunted. "This is not a matter I can decide immediately. Miss—Colonel Boyd. However, I will think on it and give you a decision within the hour."

"Who was the woman who pretended to be you?" Sylvie put in.

"As I told you last night, a brothel keeper who did some work for us in the war," Belle answered. "Her name is Eve Caterham. Probably she hoped to make money from you, General, by saying she was me. I will find out when she recovers and it will amuse me to have her as my servant."

"She's yours," Caillard stated.

"How soon can you hand over the forging plates?" von Bulow continued.

"I will make arrangements for them to be collected," Belle promised. *"After* I have settled accounts with Tollinger and Barmain."

"If you will wait in your room, Colonel," Caillard said, standing up but not offering to return the money. "I'll send for you when I've reached a decision."

"Very well," Belle answered, rising and saluting, actions which stabbed agony through her.

Turning on her heels, the girl marched from the room without a backward glance. Her whole being expressed the belief that her offer would be readily and gratefully accepted. Exchanging admiring grins, the Kid and his father followed her.

"Whooee!" breathed the Kid as they left the office and walked across the hall. "You couldn't've shook them any more if you'd walked up and slapped that blond girl in the face with a sockful of bull droppings."

"I may do it yet," Belle replied. "I don't like her and she doesn't like me."

"Thing being, will Caillard say 'yes' or 'no,'" Ysabel drawled. "They sure looked uneasy when they heard what you're after, Belle."

"I know," Belle agreed. "Did you see anything of the men from the *Posada del Infernales* last night, Sam?"

"Sure. Hoxley, their boss, backed our play to keep them *pelados* offen the Yankee gal. Had a talk with him. Seems like Tollinger hired him and the others up North after their regiment'd disbanded."

With the war ended, the Union was wasting no time in reducing its Army's size. Many men, unsettled by four years of fighting, would have no desire to return home and might leap at the offer of employment by a revolutionary general.

"Why did he help you?" Belle wanted to know. "Did he know Eve?"

"Not's he let on," Ysabel admitted. "Allowed he wouldn't see no white woman raped by greasers 'n' Injuns. Could be he told the truth."

"Did he say why he jumped us at the *posada*?" Belle asked.

"Laid the blame for it on the jasper Lon killed," Ysabel replied. "We was getting along so all-fired well I didn't push it any further."

"You did the right thing," Belle stated. "Let's wait and see what Caillard decides."

"Why don't you go rest in your room until he sends for you, Belle?" the Kid suggested. "Pappy 'n' me'll nose round a mite."

"You don't need to impress us," Ysabel went on. "We know you're one tough lil gal. I'll bet Caillard and the Austrian figure it now."

"That's what I want them to think." Belle smiled. "I'll do what you say."

Leaving the Ysabels, she went upstairs and found the two old-timers still seated outside her room. Cactus told her that nobody had tried to enter, then asked how she had got on. Quickly Belle went over what had happened downstairs and received her listeners' unqualified approbation and support.

"Count on us to back your play, Miss Belle," Rache declared. "Now you go 'n' rest up a spell. We'll stick around here and make sure you don't get bothered."

"Thanks," Belle answered gratefully. "Have you heard anything from Eve?"

"Who?" Rache grunted.

"The woman I fought last night."

"She ain't showed, nor made no noise," Cactus declared. "Who air she?"

"Danged if I see why you're doing it for her," Rache stated, after Belle had told them Eve's true identity and the story which they should give if anybody else inquired.

"I'm not sure myself," Belle admitted wryly and entered her room.

Closing the door, Belle noticed that Eve's blankets no longer had an occupant. More significant, the holster of the girl's gun belt was empty. Even as the two facts struck home, Belle heard a soft gasp of pain from the left side of the door and the barrel of her Dance jabbed into her ribs.

12
THEY'D KNOW WAYS TO
MAKE YOU TALK

"Put it down, Coniston," Belle said gently, standing still. "As soon as you pull the trigger, my friends will burst in and you'll be dead. If I'd wanted that, I could have let it happen last night."

Looking around the room while she spoke, Belle could see no sign of Eve having searched her trunks. Advancing two strides, the girl turned slowly without the revolver driving a bullet into her. Wearing a dark blue blouse and black skirt, barefoot and disheveled, her face showing something of the torment she was enduring, Eve kept the Dance's barrel pointing in Belle's direction. Despite the hammer being in the fully cocked position, Belle extended her left hand.

Dropping her eyes to the hand, Eve lifted them again to the girl's face. A mixture of admiration crept into the haggard lines of the woman's features. Aware of her own physical condition, she guessed that Belle must be suffering almost as much from the after-effects of the fight. Yet the girl stood, balancing lightly on the balls of her feet, hiding her feelings.

No fool, Eve realized that she owed her life to the Rebel Spy. If Belle, or her companions, had not intervened after the fight,

Eve would be dead now—or wishing that she was. Those same companions, at least one of whom stood outside the door, would certainly shoot her, if nothing worse, if she pulled the trigger.

"I could most likely take it," Belle remarked, reading the woman's indecision correctly. "But I'd rather you gave it back without that."

"How much do you want to say that I'm you, Boyd?" Eve demanded, without lowering the revolver. "I could pay a high price if you'd do it."

"Even if I trusted you Yankee spies," Belle replied, "why should I do it?"

Eve did not answer for a few seconds. Frowning, she looked at the girl as well as she could through the blackened, puffy slits of her eyes. Then she turned the Dance's muzzle, lowered its hammer and reversed it to lay the butt on Belle's offered palm. Releasing the weapon as Belle took hold, Eve hobbled painfully across the room and flopped onto the bed.

"All right, Boyd," Eve said. "Let's talk straight to each other."

"You first," Belle requested, walking over and returning the Dance to its holster. Drawing up a chair, she sat astride it with the gun belt hanging before her over its back.

"Why?" Eve asked.

"Last night should have answered *that,*" Belle stated.

"I've more to lose than you have," Eve pointed out. "By now they're satisfied that you're the Rebel Spy." She threw a calculating glance at the girl. "And I suppose they know who I am."

"They do," Belle agreed and, ignoring Eve's exclamation of anger, continued, "If they believe me, you are Eve Caterham, the madam of a brothel, and used to supply us with information —I thought I'd better give you a character you could play."

"Thank you, I don't think!" Eve sniffed, but her smile fought to return.

"The Yankees ran you out and you came down here hoping, by pretending to be me, to get hired as a spy."

"That's what you told Caillard?"

"All but the past part. I couldn't be expected to know that much, could I?"

"What happens now?"

"I'm keeping you here as my maid," Belle informed Eve with a smile. "I *hope* you enjoy being in my employment."

"I'll try to give satisfaction, ma'am," Eve promised, attempting to sound humble. "Why *did* you come, Boyd?"

"You'd better get into the habit of calling me 'Miss Boyd,' " Belle warned.

"Yes, *Miss* Boyd. But why—?"

"With the war over, I'm unemployed. So I've come with the Texans to enlist in General Caillard's revolutionary army. But I want to hear your side first. Talk, Coniston. I can always tell Caillard the truth and let *him* learn why you're here."

"In which case, you'd have to explain why you lied to him in the first place, *Miss* Boyd."

"All right," Belle countered. "I'll have Big Sam and the Kid take you out of the fort. They'd know ways to make you talk."

Remembering all she had heard about the Ysabel family, Eve could not hold back a slight shiver.

"They'd do it if you told them," the woman admitted. "Lord! I wish I could have worked with men who had that kind of loyalty. Listen, B—Miss Boyd, you're mistaken about Caillard."

"In what way?"

"His family have always been stout Bonapartists. And he's not a renegade planning to set up his own little kingdom."

"Go on."

"He's still loyal to Maximilian."

"You're saying this revolution business is only a scheme to weaken Juárez by drawing away men who are disaffected with his regime?"

"That's part of it. But I've been sent to learn if there's a deeper motive."

"Couldn't Major Allen trust Tollinger and Barmain to find out?" Belle asked, watching carefully for any sign of emotion to her question.

"So that's why you're here, Boyd!" Eve hissed. "I'd heard rumors that you'd sworn to kill them. Are they coming here?"

"You mean you didn't know?" Belle said cynically.

"I knew somebody would come, but not who it would be," Eve replied. "It could be you've saved my life again, B—Miss Boyd. And if you want them so badly, you'll be willing to work along with me."

"Keep talking," Belle ordered.

"What do you know about the assassination of President Lincoln?" Eve asked, settling herself comfortably on the bed.

"Only what I read in the newspapers. And the fact that our organization didn't send Booth to do it."

"*We* never thought you did, although we naturally encouraged the newspapers to make the accusation. You'd have done the same."

"Probably," Belle grunted.

"Booth and his accomplices were Southern fanatics," Eve elaborated. "But they weren't acting in the interests of the Confederate States when they murdered Lincoln. Your high brass knew that he was too wise and tolerant to impose the conditions and penalties demanded by the Northern soft-shells."

"So?"

"So I think that some of the soft-shells arranged for Booth to be persuaded to kill him and even left the way open for the attempt to be carried out."

"There either had to be bad management, or help, for Booth to get through," Belle admitted. "But—"

"But you don't see what it has to do with Caillard," Eve finished for her. "Maybe nothing. Except that things haven't gone the soft-shells' way since the end of the war. General Grant and other moderates are gaining power. Men who are willing to forget the war and let the South rebuild its economy, even if that means pardoning Confederate leaders."

"I've heard about it," Belle said. "They've refused to put our leaders on trial even."

"Which doesn't suit the soft-shells as you can imagine," Eve replied. "General Handiman's taken over the Secret Service, now that Allan Pinkerton's retired. He—and I—believe that some of the soft-shells are involved in a plot to either discredit or overthrow the moderates."

"Tollinger and Barmain, you mean?"

"They're evidently in it, along with General Smethurst and his crowd. You know of him?"

"He ran your prisoner-of-war camps," Belle answered. "Fortunately, our paths never crossed."*

"Your Captain Fog pulled some of that crowd's fangs when he killed Horace Trumpeter in Little Rock,"† Eve told Belle. "It's a pity that he didn't get more of them."

Belle had heard of the events leading up to General Trumpeter's death at the hands of Dusty Fog,‡ then a captain in the Texas Light Cavalry and soon to gain legendary status as a trail-driving, gunfighting cowhand. She had been on two missions with him§ and in the near future he would share with Mark Counter in changing the course of the Ysabel Kid's life.

"From what we can learn, but can't prove, Smethurst's crowd are conspiring with the French to place our Congress in an embarrassing situation—" Eve went on when the girl did not speak.

"*Your* Congress," Belle corrected. "I've sworn no oath of allegiance—"

"Damn it, Boyd!" Eve snapped, trying to rise but subsiding with a gasp and a wince of pain. "If they succeed, they might get into office and you know what *that* will mean to the South."

"I do," Belle confirmed, lips tightening at the thought. "What's the game?"

"From what I've learned, it's for Maximilian to be able to claim that the United States sent agents to seduce members of the French Army from their duty. Naturally, Congress will refute the claim. Then the French will be in a position to de-

* They eventually crossed, as is told in *The Hooded Riders*.
† Told in *Kill Dusty Fog!*
‡ Dusty Fog's history is told in the author's floating outfit stories.
§ Told in *The Colt and the Sabre* and *The Rebel Spy*.

mand that we show proof of our goodwill by giving active support against the *Juáristas,* which will mean open war with Mexico. If we refuse, the French will declare war on us. And that could easily bring Britain or other European countries in as France's allies."

"It might at that," Belle agreed, having followed Eve's reasoning and matched it with her own knowledge of foreign policies. "Some of the European powers would jump at an excuse to gain a foothold in America. But what will the soft-shells gain if that happens?"

"The voters up North are sickened with war," Eve explained. "They'd not stand for a government that let them be drawn into another one. Naturally the soft-shells will preach peace, lay the blame on Grant and the moderates for the war and they'll probably be in a position to end it. If that happens, they'll be in control. And I don't need to tell *you* what that will mean to white folks in the South."

"I can imagine," Belle admitted quietly. "God! There's nothing so bigoted, intolerant or out-and-out vicious than a liberal intellectual with anybody who won't conform blindly to his beliefs."

"Things haven't come to a boil ye—"

The sound of voices being raised in the passage outside Belle's door caused Eve to stop speaking.

"Get out of my way, damn you!" Sylvie Caillard was shouting, her normally sultry voice strident with anger. "My husband will have you whipped for this impertinence."

If the threat carried any weight, Cactus' even drawl showed no sign of it as he answered, speaking louder than necessary so that Belle would be able to hear.

"Colonel Boyd's resting, ma'am. I'll just sort of knock and ask if she'll see you-all."

"Go and see what the noise is about, Caterham!" Belle barked, loud enough for her words to reach the passage. "Move yourself, you idle whore, or I'll kick some life into you."

"You're enjoying this, aren't you?" Eve whispered as she rose and Belle went to lie on the bed.

Limping across to the door, Eve opened it. Outside, Cactus and Rache confronted Sylvie. The blonde's face was almost purple with fury at their disrespectful behavior. Although Cactus looked over his shoulder, neither he nor Rache offered to move. Instead, the taller Texan went through the pretense of announcing the woman's desire to speak with Colonel Boyd. Upholding the deception, Eve relayed the message. On receiving Belle's permission for Madame Caillard to enter, the men stepped aside. Storming between Cactus and Rache, Sylvie brushed by Eve and stamped indignantly into the room.

"My dear Madame Caillard," Belle purred, rising languidly. "I apologize for my men keeping you waiting. Caterham, a chair for madame. Or may I call you 'Sylvie'?"

Watching Sylvie while closing the door and fetching the chair, Eve took malicious pleasure at the blonde's obvious annoyance.

"My husband has reached a decision," Sylvie gritted, ignoring the chair and Belle's blatantly insincere welcome. "He accepts your offer."

"On my terms?" Belle asked.

"He promises that he won't intervene between you and—the men," Sylvie replied and scowled at Eve. "Has this bitch told you why she came here?"

"Tell Madame Caillard what you've just told me, Caterham!" Belle commanded. "Spit it out, or you'll get more of what I gave you last night."

Looking convincingly frightened and cowed, Eve repeated the story Belle had suggested. Belle watched Sylvie all the time and felt convinced that the blonde accepted the story. However, it raised another point and Sylvie turned suspicious eyes to the girl.

"Why didn't you let the men have her last night?"

"Because I wanted to know what her game was," Belle answered. "And I decided it would be amusing as well as useful to have her for my maid. Does the general want to see me?"

"Later today," Sylvie replied and her disapproval was obvious. "He said you might wish to rest first."

"I don't, but he's probably got arrangements to make," Belle said and raised her right leg. "Pull my boots off, Caterham. You can clean them and my belt, and be sure you do a good job of them."

"Yes'm," Eve replied humbly.

"My husband also feels that you should make arrangements for us to obtain the forging plates even if things go wrong between you and the men," Sylvie declared coldly, watching Eve straddle Belle's legs and draw off the boot. "It is not an unreasonable request."

"Probably not," Belle replied. "Anyway, I'll tell *him* what I decide when we next meet."

Giving a sniff of indignation at the curt dismissal, Sylvie turned and left the room. Smiling a little, Eve tugged off Belle's other boot. After the blonde had left, Rache looked in.

"Everything all right, Miss Belle?" he inquired, favoring Eve with a malevolent scowl.

"Yes," Belle replied. "We're hired. Will one of you stay on guard while the other fetches Sam and Lon, please?"

"I'll send me assistant," Rache promised and withdrew, closing the door.

"What was all that about?" Eve inquired. "Between you and Caillard, I mean."

"I offered to replace Tollinger and Barmain," Belle explained. "It looks as if they've taken me up on it."

"Why?" Eve demanded.

"Probably they feel that I, the Ysabels and the other two Texans have more to offer," Belle answered and described the concessions she had made in return for a chance to settle accounts with her enemies.

Eve still did not look satisfied. Frowning a little as she sat on the bed, she said, "But why would Caillard do it? I could understand him wanting money, but not forged bills."

"Unless he's planning to double-cross the French," Belle suggested.

"How do you mean?" Eve asked.

"Suppose he's considering setting up his own private kingdom after all?" Belle answered. "He might have decided that it beats being a general in the French army. Especially seeing that he has so much going for him already."

"His family are noted for their Bonapartist sympathies," Eve reminded her.

"Perhaps he feels the time's come for a change," Belle offered. "Or Sylvie may have persuaded him to do it. She looks the kind who wouldn't be slow to see the advantages of their situation. They've an all but impregnable fort, sufficient men to take and hold a large section of land. And now I'm offering them the means of arming and hiring more men. It could have made Caillard decide to become a renegade."

"I suppose it could," Eve agreed, then looked quizzically at the girl. "What do you intend to do?"

"Play along with them. Learn all I can. Then, when the time comes, I'll make my move."

"What move?"

"Settle accounts with Tollinger and Barmain."

"And after you've done it?" Eve demanded.

"I'll face up to *that* when the time comes," Belle stated. "Until then, we'll carry on as we've started. If you try to double-cross me, Coniston, I'll make you wish we'd let the men have you."

"All right," Eve replied, looking straight into Belle's eyes. "And to set things straight between us, Boyd, if I find that you're endangering the safety of the United States, I'll do my damnedest to stop you. Even if I have to kill you to do it."

13
THROW THE SWORD
AWAY, BOYD

"Senorita Colonel," the pretty little Mexican *cantinière* said, intercepting Belle as she approached the rear entrance of the mess hall to join the other guests for supper. *"Cabrito* wants you to meet him on the east wall. He says it is very important."

Ten days had gone by since Belle's eventful arrival at Fort Mendez. During that time, she and the Texans had been treated as honored guests. They had been permitted to walk about the fort, with no restrictions being placed on their movements. In return for Caillard's promise that he would allow Belle to deal with Tollinger and Barmain without interference, she had written details of how to obtain the forging equipment. Tearing the paper in half, she had given one portion to the general and retained the other until after the affair was concluded. Nothing the girl had seen or heard after that had supplied proof that Eve was correct about Caillard's motives. Nor could Belle honestly claim that he had openly declared himself as a revolutionary and renegade.

On the morning after the fight, von Bulow had ordered that all the cannon's barrels be withdrawn so that they no longer protruded beyond the embrasures. Inspecting the defenses later, in the company of the Austrian, Belle had noticed that each piece was not only kept loaded, but had its friction primer, with the firing lanyard attached, fitted in position. Pyramids of cannonballs were heaped on the ground below each cannon's mounting. She had been unable to determine whether this was standard procedure, or a precaution taken to ensure the garrison could meet an attack in the event of Caillard defecting.

Throughout the period, while the girl recovered from her injuries and exertions, there had been meetings with the *bandido* leaders which she and the Texans also attended. Caillard had talked broadly about his plans, offered substantial shares in the loot gained during his conquests and hinted at arms and ammunition being forthcoming, but he had made no attempt to implement activity in his proposed revolution. As food and drink continued to flow freely, the various delegations raised no objections. A few Mexican intellectuals arrived and departed, their interviews with Caillard being conducted in secret.

Cultivating Hoxley's men, Belle had soon reached the conclusion that they knew nothing of their employers' plans. Hoxley expressed open admiration for her and stuck to his story that Kansas and *Cicatriz* alone had been responsible for the attack on the Kid at the *Posada del Infernales*. Not that Belle had expected him to admit otherwise and she did not press the matter.

Turning Sylvie's unpopularity to her advantage, Belle had won over most of the garrison, from *cantinières* to hard-bitten veterans. Showing none of *madame la générale*'s arrogant, bad-tempered snobbery, Belle had captivated the junior officers. Once the stiffness had left her muscles, she had made regular visits to the *salle d'armes* where she further stole Sylvie's thunder by demonstrating her skill at fencing. Although good herself, the blonde had repeatedly refused to cross swords with the girl and lost face by doing so. Nothing Belle had learned led her to believe that the garrison officers, except possibly von Bulow, had access to Caillard's schemes. Also mingling on good terms with the soldiers, the Texans had proved equally unsuccessful in their findings.

Hoping to provoke Sylvie into indiscretion, Belle had openly flirted with von Bulow. While the blonde did not hide her annoyance, she had failed to react as Belle had hoped she would. Discussing the matter with Eve—who continued to play the dispirited, beaten and sullen maid—and the Texans, Belle had concluded that Caillard might be waiting for Tollinger and Barmain to arrive before reaching a decision on which line to take.

The only other item of note had been the interest Caillard and the various gang leaders had shown in the money that Belle had been under orders to deliver to General Klatwitter. The more Belle and her companions insisted that it had been destroyed, the greater had been the disbelief displayed by their questioners. So far, however, there had been no more than hints. Nobody was foolish enough to try to forcibly extract the location of the "buried" wealth.

Knowing the *cantinière* to be a very close friend of the Kid's, Belle did not question her about the message. Thanking her, the girl went out of the main building. With a new moon rising, the night was not too dark and Belle's eyes soon became accustomed to it. Left hand resting lightly on the hilt of her sheathed rapier, she strode in the direction of the east wall. Studying it, she saw an indistinct shape standing alongside one of the cannon and looking through the embrasure. Further along the terreplein, a second figure she assumed to be a sentry was also looking out of the fort. Belle wondered why the Kid had sent for her. Perhaps he had seen something of interest and, wishing to keep it under observation, had asked her to come instead of joining her in the mess hall.

Going up the steps, Belle walked along the terreplein. Beyond the cannon, the dark shape continued to look through the embrasure. Footsteps echoed hollowly as the second figure came toward her. Then, as she drew level with the cannon, the girl realized that the footfalls lacked the solid thud of heavy infantry boots and the man making them walked with a mincing gait that had not been induced by parade-ground drilling. Peering more carefully, she became aware that the approaching man neither wore a uniform nor carried a rifle.

"Lon?" Belle hissed, reaching with her right hand toward the rapier's hilt and wishing that she had strapped on her revolver.

"Guess again, Boyd," answered a mocking voice that sounded nothing like the Ysabel Kid's pleasant tenor drawl.

With a growing sense of shock, Belle watched the man by the cannon turn her way. Up that close, she could see that he wore a derby hat, town suit and a collarless white shirt. In his right hand, a small revolver was aimed directly at her stomach. Recognition came instantly and the girl tensed ready to leap to the attack.

"Tollinger!" Belle hissed, and the one word throbbed with pent-up hatred.

Although the second man on the eastern terreplein started to run in her direction, Belle knew that she could expect no help from that source. Given so much of a clue, she had identified the stocky shape of Barmain during a swift glance flickered away from Tollinger.

"We've got her, Alfie," Barmain enthused in the high-pitched, affected tone which had always set Belle's teeth on edge.

"We've got her, Georgie," Tollinger agreed, then his voice hardened. "Throw the sword away, Boyd."

All too well Tollinger and Barmain remembered the way Belle had handled a rapier during the attack on her home. Two of their drunken rabble had gone down, spitted by the flashing blade in the hands of the slim, beautiful girl. So Tollinger wanted to remove such a deadly weapon from her reach.

At first Belle considered refusing, sliding the blade from its sheath and staking all in a sudden lunge. Cold logic came in time to prevent her from making the attempt. Tollinger was standing much too far away for the girl to hope to reach him and prevent the revolver firing. Barmain had come to a halt at an equally safe distance. So she knew that she must obey, playing for a respite in the hope that something might happen to give her a chance of survival.

Perhaps somebody might come from the casemate beneath their feet, although that was a slender hope, the eastern wall being given over to storerooms. Maybe one of the garrison or guests would walk by. Possibly the sentries on the north or south walls might become suspicious and come to investigate. Belle knew that refusal to comply with the demand meant death; and while life remained, there was the hope of a rescue. So she slowly lowered her hands, unbuckled her belt and let it fall at her feet.

"Kick it over the edge," Tollinger ordered.

"I see that you've still got the same wife, *Alfie*," Belle sneered as she sent the belt and its burden sliding over the edge of the terreplein.

An angry snarl rumbled from Barmain's lips, for he deeply resented the girl's mocking reference to his homosexual relationship with Tollinger. However, it did not produce the effect for which it had been made. Clenching his fists, Barmain continued to stand beyond her reach.

"You've made a lot of trouble for us, Boyd," Tollinger gritted.

"And caused some of our friends to be killed," Barmain went on.

"You'll soon find fresh bedmates, Georgie," Belle answered, but once again she failed to produce the required response. "What now, Tollinger?"

"We heard that you want to kill us," Tollinger replied. "So we're going to protect ourselves by killing you first."

"With a gun?" Belle scoffed. "The shot will bring the guard out, and the rest of the garrison. I wouldn't give much for your chances of survival when my friends find out you've shot me."

"She promised us that they'll be taken care of," Barmain spat out, darting a nervous glance toward the main building.

"But can you trust her?" Belle countered, guessing at which "she" the soft-shell meant and playing on his suspicious nature. "There are more than the Texans I can call my friends, including a number of the garrison. *She* might not arrive quickly enough to stop some of them blowing your stupid Yankee heads off."

"She could be right, Alfie!" Barmain wavered. "We'll have to kill her quietly and get away from the wall before anybody knows it's happened."

"You're right, Georgie," Tollinger admitted and slipped the revolver into his waistband. Dipping his hand into the jacket's pocket, he produced and started to open a long-bladed folding knife.

"If you're going to kill me, *Georgie,* I'll turn around," Belle mocked at him. "That's the only way you'd have the guts to kill even a woman," Exhibiting an attitude of complete disdain, she began to pivot toward the edge of the terreplein. "Come on, you rotten, cowardly swish. I'll make it easy for you!"

"Swish!" Barmain screeched, knowing it to be the derogatory term for homosexual. "I'll—"

Words failed the soft-shell. At last the goad of Belle's icy contempt and mockery of his effeminate nature had pricked home. Spluttering off into an incoherent gurgle, he lunged at the girl and his hands drove almost womanlike in the direction of her hair. In doing so, Barmain played straight into her hands.

From a slow start, Belle spun swiftly around on her left foot. Tilting her torso away from Barmain's reaching fingers, she raised and swung her right leg. With a power increased by the momentum of her turn, she propelled the toe of her boot into her attacker's side. A croak of pain burst from Barmain as the kick landed. Staggering, he gyrated and reached the edge of the terreplein while going backward. Feeling himself falling, he let out a shriek. Down he went, his spine colliding with the uppermost of a pile of cannonballs. Bone crackled, sounding hideously clear in the silence that followed as agony stilled Barmain's voice. Sliding down the pyramid, his body contorted spasmodically in torment for a few seconds. Then it became limp and still.

With his knife's blade open, Tollinger froze momentarily at

the sight of his friend tumbling backward from the terreplein. Letting out a snarl that sounded a good half fear, he lunged in the girl's direction. From kicking Barmain, Belle brought her right foot down. Using it to pivot on, she faced Tollinger, took aim and whipped up her left leg. Flying accurately, her boot struck beneath the man's thrusting knife hand. Tollinger yelped as his arm snapped upward, his fingers opened and the knife flew from them to pass over the parapet.

Bringing down her left foot, Belle slashed a savage punch. It caught the side of Tollinger's jaw and caused him to retreat. For all that, he recovered fast. As the girl followed him up, he brought himself to a halt and whirled a backhand blow to her head that knocked her sprawling. The wall prevented Belle from going down. Hanging against it with her head spinning, she saw Tollinger looming toward her. Before she could regain her equilibrium, he had reached her and his fingers closed about her neck.

Spitting curses, his face distorted with rage and fright, Tollinger tightened his hold. Choked by the grip, Belle grabbed at his wrists and kicked savagely. Although unable to put all her strength into the efforts, the impact of her boots upon Tollinger's shins still hurt. Almost gibbering with the pain, he dragged the girl forward and slammed her against the wall. Belle's moan was strangled into a faint hiss by the clutching hands. Again and again she kicked, raining the attacks against the sensitive area of his shins. Incoherent mutters rose from him and he swung the girl around. Trying to keep his legs clear of her driving boots, he attempted to force her across the terreplein.

Desperately Belle spiked the heels of her boots into the hard-packed earth surface of the terreplein. Such was the strength in her slender frame that she forced Tollinger to halt in the center of the level area. Mindful of the girl's savage assault on his shins, he concentrated most of his attention on keeping his legs away from her feet. Maintaining his hold on the girl's neck, he opened his feet and edged them to the rear.

Belle did not kick straight away. Like a flash she caught his left wrist from above with her right hand. Equally swiftly, she passed her left hand over his right arm to join its mate on the trapped limb. Already feeling the need for air, she exerted all her will to continue with what she hoped would prove an escape from the danger of strangulation. With the hold gained, she arched her torso away from him almost like a contortionist performing a back bend. Not until then did she kick. Up drove her right foot, its toe passing between his separated thighs in the direction of his crotch. Although the speed with which she moved precluded the full use of her power, the kick still landed hard enough for her purposes. Tollinger did not release her throat, but she felt his fingers slacken. That was all the girl asked for.

Gratefully dragging air into her throbbing lungs, she twisted her body sharply to the left. Regaining her hold on the wrist, she thrust downward with her left elbow and used its leverage against his right arm to wrench her neck free. Continuing to turn until her back was toward him, she carried and held the trapped limb under her right armpit. Doing so caused Tollinger to bend forward and she leaned to the rear so that her weight rested on his left shoulder.

Respiration restored, Belle went ahead with her escape. Gathering herself, she threw her legs into the air and rolled backward over Tollinger's shoulders. On landing, giving him no chance to straighten up, she turned his arm free and brought up her bent right leg. Smashing into the center of his face, Belle's knee lifted the soft-shell erect. Blood gushed from his nostrils as he reeled away from her. Turning from the force of the attack, he plunged alongside the cannon toward the embrasure.

Never had the simple, involuntary process of breathing felt so pleasant to Belle as during the seconds immediately following her escape from Tollinger's fingers. Stumbling slightly, she caught her balance. About to follow the reeling man and render him incapable of further efforts, she saw that he was in the process of averting the danger.

Throwing his left arm across the barrel of the cannon, he clutched at it. Feet teetering on the lip of the embrasure, he managed to halt his advance and turn inward. Doing so brought his chest around until it rested against the muzzle of the piece. Pain and terror tore at him. Being what he was, his self-centered ego recognized only one thing. He gave no thought to the threat to his mission, or avenging his friend. All he wanted to do was escape from the girl. Yet he knew that he must also try to kill her. Even should he flee from the fort unscathed, he would never know a secure minute as long as Belle Boyd lived. With that in mind, still clinging to and leaning against the cannon's barrel, he grabbed at his revolver and the fingers of his free hand closed about its butt.

Even as she sprang forward, Belle knew that she could not get to Tollinger before he completed his draw. So she did not try. Instead she grabbed the priming compound and with the rough surface of the iron striker ignited the highly combustible substance. Flame flashed from the friction primer through the vent hole and detonated the ten pounds of black powder that formed the main charge. Turning into a vast mass of gas, the charge thrust a solid lead ball, seven inches in diameter and weighing 42.7 pounds, along the ten-foot-nine-inch-long smoothbore tube. Emerging, it struck Tollinger—who stood well within the 1,955 yards maximum range—and blasted him, revolver still not lined on the girl, from in front of the muzzle.

Avoiding the piece's wicked recoil slam, Belle let the lanyard fall from her fingers. The murder of her parents had been at least partially avenged. Maybe fully, for she had heard and seen nothing of Barmain after he fell from the wall. Bracing herself on the breech of the cannon, Belle fought down the nausea that threatened to engulf her.

Voices rose, shouting questions or comments, as the thunderous roar of the cannon shattered the air. Pouring out of their room by the main gate, the off-duty members of the guard rushed toward the source of the disturbance. The sentries on the north and south walls converged on the double, racing along the terreplein with rifles at the ready. A stream of men and women burst out of the mess hall. Soldiers quit their quarters in the casement's rooms.

Already suspicious at Belle's nonarrival in the hall, the four Texans led the rush. Racing across the barrack square ahead of the others, the Kid looked to where Belle was walking slowly down the terreplein stairs.

"What the hell?" growled the youngster, staring from the girl to the shape of the pyramid of cannonballs. "How— Why—?"

"Somebody lied to me," Belle replied and looked to where a soldier was shining a lantern's light on Barmain. In French she continued, "Is he dead?"

Kneeling by the still figure, the sergeant of the guard answered, *"Oui, mon colonel.* I think his back is broken." He used the formal mode of address without any hint of sarcasm, speaking as politely as if addressing one of his own officers. "Did you—?"

"Oui," Belle agreed. "He and his friend tried to kill me."

"That's one of 'em, huh?" growled the Kid. Although unable to follow the conversation between Belle and the sergeant, he guessed what had happened. Reaching for his knife, he went on, "Is the other son of a bitch around?"

"No," Belle replied quietly. "I shot him."

Vociferous chatter rose in three languages as Belle's words were relayed or translated through the crowd. A bellow brought the torrent of French exclamations to a ragged halt as Caillard and von Bulow made their belated appearance. Watching the two senior officers force a way through the crowd, Belle noticed that Sylvie was not with them. That came as a surprise, for the girl would have expected the blonde to come and discover the result of the fight. Everything pointed to Sylvie having organized the meeting, yet she seemed to be displaying a surprising lack of interest in its outcome.

"What happened, Colonel Boyd?" Caillard demanded, watching one of the guard gather up and return the girl's weapon belt to her.

"Somebody laid a trap for me," Belle answered as she buckled on the belt. "It didn't work."

"A trap!" Caillard repeated and his shock appeared genuine

enough. Throwing a look at von Bulow, who maintained an air of icy, calm, detached innocence, the general seemed to be on the verge of making further comment. With an almost visible struggle, he refrained from doing so. Instead he glared around and barked in French, "Back to your quarters, all of you. Sergeant of the guard, clear this area and return your men to their duties. Doctor, see if that one is dead and remove him. Is the other here, Colonel Boyd?"

"No," the girl replied. "He was standing in front of the cannon when I fired it."

"Then we needn't worry about him," Caillard said indifferently.

"Gentlemen," von Bulow remarked in Spanish, the inevitable sneer in his voice as he made use of the honorific mode of address to the guests. "If you return to the main hall, food and *drink* will be waiting."

Discipline drove away the French soldiers, except for the surgeon's party. After making certain that Barmain was dead, he asked Belle if she required his professional services. On being told that she did not, he told his assistants to carry the body away. Guessing that there would be few, if any, further developments to interest them, the guests headed back to their interrupted feeding and drinking in the mess hall. Only the four Texans remained. Ignoring the scowls directed at them by Caillard and von Bulow, they formed a grim-faced, uncompromising half circle behind the slender girl.

"Did you know those two bastards'd got here, General?" Ysabel growled.

"No!" Caillard barked and, again, Belle believed that he spoke the truth. "Did you, Otto?"

"They arrived just before we closed the gates at sunset, *mon général,*" von Bulow replied. "I had them quartered in one of the casemate rooms, wishing to avoid an incident until after I had spoken to you about them. But I couldn't get you alone to speak privately."

Ysabel could not argue with that point. At no time during the evening had Caillard been separated from his guests.

Clearly the various *bandido* leaders were becoming restive and wanted some definite action. None of them being willing to trust the others, they had swarmed around the general all evening. If von Bulow was sensitive to atmosphere, he might have hesitated to ask Caillard to leave the men for a private conversation.

About to take the matter further, Belle saw Sylvie hurrying across the parade ground. The girl's lips tightened and her right hand rested on the rapier's hilt as she prepared to challenge the blonde with being implicated in the trap. Coming up to the group, Sylvie gave Belle no chance of doing so.

"Thank God you're safe, M—Colonel Boyd!" the blonde ejaculated.

Instantly Belle's suspicions increased. Until that moment, Sylvie had steadfastly refused to address her by her military rank. The lantern held by von Bulow did not give sufficient illumination for Belle to see Sylvie's face clearly. It almost seemed that the blonde was standing away from the light.

"Didn't you think I would be?" Belle countered coldly.

"I didn't know what to think. When I heard that the two men had reached the fort and you didn't come to dinner, I became suspicious. So I went to your room to make sure all was well with you. That Caterham woman was quarreling with one of the *cantinières* about how much she should pay for the girl luring you out here to Tollinger and Barmain."

"Where are they now?" Belle asked.

"Caterham knifed the girl before I could get into the room and stop her," Sylvie answered. "I had to run her through with my sword when she tried to kill me. There was no other way of doing it. Caterham is dead."

14
YOU'LL PAY THE PRICE
OF FAILURE

"What do we do now, Belle?" asked the Ysabel Kid as the Texans and the girl returned to the fort after Eve Coniston's funeral.

Although the Rebel Spy had exhibited an attitude of indifference, or at most annoyance at being deprived of a maid, her companions sensed the hidden grief that filled her. Through the days following their latest meeting, Belle had formed a growing admiration and respect for the Yankee agent. Suffering far worse than the girl from the after-effects of the fight, Eve had never once forgotten to play her part. Every day she had served Belle's breakfast in bed, washed and pressed the girl's clothes. When in Sylvie's presence, Belle had treated Eve like dirt and piled indignities on her in the hope that the blonde would make advances to a possible ally. Working to the same end, Eve had heaped vituperation on her "employer's" head in Belle's absence. In the end, that had worked to Sylvie's advantage.

Going to Caillard's office the previous night, Belle's party had attended the inquiry that the general had insisted in holding. Brought from his post, the guard commander had explained why his sentries had failed to prevent the fight. The dead *cantinière* had delivered a message, claiming it to have originated from Caillard, ordering him to remove the man from the east wall and keep the guards on the north and south terrepleins away from that area. According to the story he had been given, two of the garrison's officers intended to fight a duel and wanted privacy.

Dueling was still permitted in the French Army, but it had been restricted to the *au premier sang* fight in which the drawing of first blood, no matter how little, brought it to an end. That ruling did not meet the approval of the hot-blooded young officers. If two of them quarreled, they often settled the matter far more permanently. To avoid wrecking the winner's career, the loser's injuries would be written of as an accident. In the interests of diplomacy, such duels were invariably carried out away from possible witnesses. So the sergeant of the guard had seen nothing suspicious in his instructions. Even the *cantinière* delivering them could be classed as understandable. She would be less likely to be suspected of complicity should the duel have fatal results.

Bitterly Belle had accepted that she could not prove anything against Sylvie. Eve's threats had been recalled by the blonde, establishing a motive for her aiding the two soft-shells. It had been suggested by von Bulow that "Caterham" could have been a traitor to the South, or hired by Tollinger and Barmain after the end of the war, to account for how she had known the softshells. An examination of the women's bodies yielded nothing except proof of Sylvie's thoroughness. The *cantinière* had been knifed in the back by a weapon still gripped in Eve's hand. Pain had so distorted Eve's face that it had wiped away the emotions she had felt an instant before the rapier pierced her heart. Every point that had occurred to Belle had also been expected, countered or explained away by the blonde. So, wisely, Belle had forced herself to make the pretense of accepting Eve's guilt.

Excusing herself from joining the other guests, Belle had retired to her room at the end of the inquiry. The bodies had already been removed and their blood washed away. Left alone, behind the locked door, Belle had sobbed long and bitterly, the first time for many a year. She had spent a very restless night. In addition to the emotional strain of having finally avenged her parents, she had felt a deep and gnawing sense of loss over Eve's death.

Despite the fact that they had twice fought each other with primitive savagery, Belle and Eve had become good friends. So much so that Eve had suggested that Belle should forget the war, swear the oath of allegiance to the Union and apply for acceptance as a member of the Yankee Secret Service. Having lost a number of its best operatives, who had retired to join a private detective force formed by Allan Pinkerton, Eve's organization could use a woman of Belle's ability.

Knowing the precarious nature of her assignment, Eve had insisted on making preparations for the worst. She had told Belle the name of her superior in Brownsville and given the girl a password that would ensure her admission to him. More than that, Eve had told the Ysabels of her offer to Belle. To her surprise, when discussing the matter, Belle found that the Texans were agreeable to her accepting it. As Sam Ysabel had said, conditions in Mexico would remain too chaotic for profitable smuggling until either the *Juaristas* or the French gained full control. So he and the Kid would go back to mustanging, catching and breaking wild horses, for a living while awaiting more settled times below the border. Belle had suspected that her male companions were relieved to know that she could find gainful, and well-paid, employment.

All that ran through Belle's head as she walked at the Kid's side and tried to decide on an answer to his question.

"You're not going to let her get away with it, are you?" the Kid demanded impatiently.

"Not if I can help it," Belle stated and her voice held a grim, purposeful note the listening men recognized. They had last heard it when she spoke of her determination to find her parents' murderers. "I'm going to make Sylvie Caillard wish that she'd never been born."

"Looks like they've decided to stay loyal to Maximilian,

Miss Belle," Cactus remarked. "They'd never've tried to set you up thataways if they didn't."

"Unless I'm sadly mistaken, that was Sylvie's idea," Belle objected. "I don't think Caillard, or von Bulow, knew anything about it."

"She'd want that forged money if they aim to set up on their own," Ysabel pointed out. "And with you dead, they'd not get the other half of that letter."

"That's why she killed Eve and the *cantinière*," Belle answered. "She knows that you know where it is, Sam. With me dead, and the people you'd blame for it killed, you would hand my half over to Caillard. It's no use to you without his part. Probably they'd have let you kill Tollinger and Barmain. Then they'd go ahead with setting up their own private kingdom."

"You mean they'd hope I'd hand it over," Ysabel corrected and the girl nodded her agreement. "How're you fixing to play it now, Belle?"

"Let's go and have a showdown with Caillard," Belle suggested. "If you're willing to gamble on me being right, that is."

"You've been right often enough for us to take a chance," drawled the Kid and the others rumbled concurrence.

"If I'm wrong this time," Belle warned, "we're all likely to get shot."

"How about if you've guessed right?" asked Ysabel.

"Not *if*," amended Rache. *"When!"*

"I stands corrected." Ysabel grinned. "What happens *when* you're right?"

"We'll have a choice," Belle replied. "Either we side him all the way, or we do what Eve wanted and save the United States from a whole mess of bad trouble."

"Eve warn't a bad gal," Rache commented. "And I don't cotton to foreigners."

"And I never did take to the notion of owning no big *hacienda*," Ysabel went on. "Man has to work a whole heap too hard running one."

On that note, the discussion ended. Passing through the gates of the fort, they went to the main building. In the small hall at the rear, they found the sergeant major and asked if they could see the general. With the minimum of delay, Belle and the Texans were ushered into the office. Flanked by his wife and von Bulow, Caillard sat behind his desk. Interest showed on the two men's faces as they stood up. Sylvie remained seated and scowled at Belle while attempting to avoid meeting the girl's eyes.

"I was just going to send for you, Colonel Boyd," Caillard declared. "Would you care to be seated?"

"That depends, General," Belle answered.

"On what?" Caillard asked, aware of the grim, businesslike note in her voice.

"On whether you intend to strike out on your own, or follow the plan your superiors made with Tollinger and Barmain's crowd."

Startled exclamations broke from the Caillards and von Bulow. Thrusting back her chair, Sylvie started to rise. Her husband's right hand snapped downward to pull open the desk's drawer. Reaching across his torso, von Bulow began to thumb open the flap of his holster. None of the hostile gestures reached fulfillment. Knowing Belle, the Texans had been ready for her to spark off a grandstand play. At the end of her speech, their hands were already resting on gun butts. Steel rasped on leather, followed by the clicking of hammers riding back to full cock and four revolvers lined across the desk. Although a Lefaucheux revolver lay in the drawer, Caillard kept his hand away from it. Freezing, von Bulow allowed his Army Colt to remain in its holster. Once more Belle locked eyes with Sylvie and the girl's sword hand tapped the rapier's hilt. Sinking back onto her chair, the blonde turned her head away.

"Put up your guns, boys," Belle said. "I'm sure the general and Count von Bulow are willing to listen to reason."

"We are," Caillard confirmed, watching the Texans' weapons return to leather. He sat down and closed the drawer of the desk. "Would you explain your comment, Colonel Boyd?"

"Certainly," Belle obliged. "Either you will make your defection a fact, or you'll pay the price of failure."

"In what way?" Sylvie spat.

"Before General Smethurst can replace Tollinger and Barmain, the Yankee Secret Service might learn what's going on," Belle replied. "And even if they don't, your high command aren't going to take kindly to learning they were killed before they could be of any use."

"You know a lot that you shouldn't!" Sylvie hissed.

"Blame Tollinger and Barmain for that," Belle said calmly. "They just couldn't resist boasting to me about what they hoped to do."

While Belle and his wife were talking, Caillard sat scowling at the top of his desk. Inadvertently, the girl had struck a nerve with her reference to his paying the price of failure. During the Napoleonic Wars, his grandfather had paid such a price. A colonel of *Gendarmerie,* and one of the Emperor's personal *aides-de-camp,* Jean-Baptiste Caillard had allowed two British naval officers to escape from his custody.* Doing so had caused Bonaparte great inconvenience and humiliation in the eyes of the world. In the tyrannical First Empire, there could be only one penalty for such an act. Colonel Caillard had been court-martialed, found guilty and shot.

If General Caillard knew anything about his rivals in the French Army, the failure of his grandfather would be remembered when he was called to answer for the ruin of a carefully laid plot to remove the menace of United States intervention. He would be lucky to avoid his grandfather's fate. That was another factor to sway him along the path that had already been suggested by his wife and von Bulow.

"We made an agreement, Colonel Boyd," Caillard announced. "As Tollinger and Barmain are dead, I have kept my part of it."

"And I'll keep mine," Belle replied, accepting the seat brought to her by the Kid.

Greed flickered on Caillard's face as the girl took out and spread her half of the letter on the desk before him. Producing

* Told in C. S. Forester's *Flying Colours.*

his section, he married the two portions. Then his head jerked up sharply.

"The forging plates are in New Orleans!"

"Of course," Belle answered calmly.

"Then how do we get them?" Sylvie spat out.

"Matt Harvey has a fast boat," the girl pointed out. "On receipt of this letter, and a password, Madam Lucienne will hand over the whole consignment."

"And, of course, Harvey will bring it back here," Sylvie mocked.

"He won't know what he's carrying," Belle replied. "Cactus, Colonel von Bulow, or another of your trusted men will accompany him, General." She flashed a look at Caillard. "There are men in the garrison you can trust?"

"There are some," Caillard admitted. "I can send one with your man and Harvey, but collecting the plates will take time."

"I agree," Belle said. "How long will we have, do you think, before your superiors become suspicious?"

"Two weeks, not more than three," Caillard guessed and von Bulow gave a confirmatory nod.

"Good," Belle enthused. "Before then, the gang leaders can have their men assembled. It will give us time to think up some reason to send away all but the trustworthy members of the garrison and make ready to repel any attack Maximilian launches."

"The gang leaders will need something more substantial than promises in the way of payment before they bring their men," von Bulow warned. "And not in French or Mexican money. That is why we hoped to get the forging equipment quickly."

"Would they accept Yankee gold?" asked Belle.

"Of cour—" the Austrian began, then he stared at the girl. "You mean the money that was to be paid to Klatwitter?"

"I do," Belle confirmed. "It could be collected and brought here in—eight days, would you say, Sam?"

"Eight days easy enough, Colonel," agreed Ysabel. "Fact being, me 'n' the boy could get it in less."

Once again Belle felt admiration at the way the big Texan had not only followed her lead, but improved upon it.

Clearly Ysabel's suggestion did not meet with the Caillards' or von Bulow's approval; not that he had expected it to. Watching the general, Belle could see him struggling to decide upon the best line of action. With fifty thousand dollars in gold at stake—the actual amount had been much less, but legend had increased the quantity—Caillard felt disinclined to trust any of his subordinates. Certainly he could not contemplate allowing the Texans to make the collection unescorted. Nor did he regard his wife or von Bulow as suitable candidates. Given that much money, either or both of them would probably slip across the border and disappear into the United States.

"Why not let Count Otto take a small escort and Sam Ysabel or the Kid to guide him?" Belle suggested, knowing that Caillard would not agree.

"Or you could come with me, General," Ysabel went on. "Colonel Belle, Lon 'n' Rache'll stay on here and help get the fort ready for a fight. Lon knows Mexicans and Injuns better'n most, he'll likely be able to tell you which way them gang leaders're really thinking."

"Eight days, you say?" Caillard breathed, looking calculating.

"Less with good horses 'n' riders," Ysabel corrected. "A cavalryman like you could maybe cut it down to six if the others don't slow us."

"Your presence would encourage greater speed, Gautier," Sylvie remarked. "Otto and I can take care of things here, with *Colonel* Boyd's help. There is one thing puzzling me, though."

"And that is?" Belle challenged, guessing the words were directed at her.

"You have killed Tollinger and Barmain," Sylvie explained. "So why are you willing to pour your own money into this venture?"

"For very good reasons," Belle answered. "I wanted my revenge, but I knew that getting it wouldn't be the end. Smethurst and his crowd won't forget that I've ruined their plans.

Nor can I use that money north of the border; it was originally looted from the Yankees. So I may as well invest it. In return, I want a good share of the profits. Sufficient money to set me up comfortably for life in Europe. I developed a taste for living there during the war."

Going by their reaction to the words, Belle had presented motives that her audience could appreciate. She saw the Caillards and von Bulow exchange glances and knowing, satisfied nods. Apparently the reasons for her participation in the defection had been debated and she had now cleared up any lingering doubts on the matter. Most likely Sylvie still did not approve of Belle's inclusion in the plan, but she was willing to accept it—at least, until such time as Belle's usefulness came to an end.

"I will see Captain Harvey straightaway," Caillard decided and looked at Cactus. "My sergeant major will accompany you, Mr. Jones."

"Count on me to take care of him, General," the old-timer promised soberly. "How soon can we go?"

"If Harvey is agreeable, you should be able to leave this afternoon," Caillard replied. "Yes, Mr. Ysabel?"

"Might be best if you got them gang leaders off afore you send any of your soldiers away, General," Ysabel suggested. "Was I you, I'd not have them knowing how many soldiers you'd got left."

"That is wise," Caillard praised. "Sylvie, my dear, we have men—and a lady—with intelligence as well as courage here."

"Yes," Sylvie sniffed shortly.

"How about the Mexican intellectuals, General?" Belle inquired. "Will they be a significant factor in our revolution?"

"I doubt it," Caillard snorted. "Like all their kind, they don't mind the meek inheriting the earth, as long as somebody else takes all the risks and does all the fighting for them to get it. They'll be of no use to us."

"That leaves Hoxley and the others Tollinger hired," von Bulow remarked.

"Don't worry about them," Belle said. "They're in this for money and will fight for us as long as they are paid for it."

"Then all we have to do is collect the money, and we are ready to win ourselves an empire," Caillard enthused.

"I can hardly wait to make a start," Belle assured him, with such sincerity that she might have been speaking the truth.

15
ARE YOU LOYAL TO FRANCE?

Sitting on her bed, nursing her Dance under the tunic draped across her knees, Belle looked at the two French *cantinières*. It would soon be evening on the day after the plot had been put into motion. Everything now depended on a question she was about to render. If she received the correct answer, her departure from Fort Mendez should become considerably easier.

Once the decision to defect had been taken, Caillard had lost no time in setting it into motion. Called into the office for a private consultation, Matt Harvey had agreed to transport Cactus and a small party of French soldiers to New Orleans, supply them with civilian clothing *en route,* then return them and their unspecified cargo to the fort.

The increase in the sergeant major's escort had been Belle's idea, ostensibly to guard against treachery on Harvey's part. In reality, she wanted to cause a further drain on Caillard's limited manpower. Pressed for information before they had interviewed Harvey, the general had admitted that he could only rely upon a small portion of the garrison. Hard, arrogant, and a martinet, Caillard possessed none of the qualities needed to inspire loyalty or devotion among his subordinates. Those he could count on to support his defection were the malcontents in search of easy promotion or wealth and others disenchanted with the latest Bonaparte to establish himself as ruler in France. They were not the material for grand conquest, but that had been a point in Belle's favor when she insisted that they should prevent the gang leaders discovering Caillard's exact fighting strength.

If presented with the opportunity, Cactus would slip away from Harvey and the sergeant major before boarding the ship. Should he be unable to do so, he would travel with them to New Orleans. Once a very capable member of the Confederate States Secret Service, Madam Lucienne—returned to her successful dress shop at the end of the war—ought to possess the means to help him escape and organize his return to Texas.

With Harvey's party dispatched, Belle had supervised the other stages of the plan. Gathering the other gang leaders, Caillard had announced that he meant to start his revolution in two weeks' time. Questioned about the reason for the delay, he had explained that he needed a respite to obtain firearms from north of the border. However, he had promised every leader an advance payment depending on the size of the contingent he brought back. Having the full force of the garrison to enforce his decisions, he received few arguments to the arrangement. Hoxley and his men had been sent to Brownsville so that they could spread the word along the border that gunfighters could find employment at Fort Mendez. By evening, all the guests had taken their departure. At Belle's insistence, the Kid had left the fort and made a wide circle around it to ensure that none of the gangs remained in the vicinity.

Soon after breakfast the next morning, bugles blew assembly and the cry of *"Aux armes!"* was bellowed. Parading ready for any eventuality, the garrison had been addressed by their general. According to Caillard, a message had just been received from the French forces holding San Luis Potosí saying that they were facing the attack of a large *Juárista* army. Reinforcements must be rushed there immediately.

The major assigned to command of the relief column had

barely been able to hide his surprise at learning that neither
Caillard nor von Bulow would accompany it. Also he had
looked dubious as he considered the wisdom of leaving the fort
so poorly manned. Caillard was keeping only fifty men, and not
the pick of the garrison. However, discipline had prevailed and
the major had held back the objections he undoubtedly felt. So
much the better, Belle had thought; he would be the more inclined to listen and believe when a messenger reached him with
information about the true state of affairs.

To Caillard's way of thinking, everything was going his way.
San Luis Potosí lay a good week's march to the west, for a force
comprised of foot soldiers, a couple of twelve-pounder gun
howitzers and a small cavalry screen. The way led through
territory where *Juárista* activity could be expected to add de-
lays. By the time the major arrived, reported and returned, Fort
Mendez would be defended by men from the various *bandido*
gangs. Already faced with a long, difficult task in subduing the
Juáristas, the French Army might easily decide to ignore the
defection until able to give it their full attention. In which case,
the revolution could go ahead.

By noon, the relief column had left the vicinity of the fort,
followed by Rache, at Belle's insistence. In the early afternoon,
Ysabel had led Caillard and ten well-mounted men to the
northeast. That left Sylvie and von Bulow with forty men and
the *cantinières.* From what Belle had seen, the blonde intended
to make sure that she and the Kid remained within the fort
until Caillard and Ysabel returned.

So Belle had decided to take a chance. Originally *cantinières*
had been mere camp followers, picking up discarded items of
regimental clothing to replace their own worn-out garments.
By the time of the Franco-Austrian War in Italy, a change had
come. The *cantinière* became an established member of the
French Army, with a uniform of regulation pattern and subject
to military discipline. Of course, some of them were no more
than prostitutes taking advantage of an assured market for
their wares, but many others were dedicated to their work and
felt as great a pride in their regiment as did its male members.

The problem facing Belle was to which category Marthe and Alice belonged.

Taking a chance, she had asked them both to come to her quarters. Sylvie had made it plain that she did not trust Belle. In the Rebel Spy's presence, the blonde had told the guard commander that *nobody*—with a pointed glance at Belle and the Kid as she laid emphasis on the word —must be allowed to leave the fort. Granted the *cantinières*' help, the girl and the young Texan hoped not only to escape, but to take their horses and property with them.

"Are you loyal to France?" Belle demanded, watching the two women's faces.

"Of course!" Marthe stated immediately and stiffened to attention as she said the words. Before doing so, she flashed a knowing look at the other *cantinière.*

"My father, husband and two brothers all gave their lives in the service of our country, Colonel," Alice went on. "Why do you ask?"

"There is treachery afoot," Belle replied. "No messenger came from San Luis Potosí—"

"Then the men have gone on a wild goose chase!" Marthe said grimly.

"Hah!" Alice ejaculated and glared triumphantly at Marthe. "I told you—"

"No more than I already suspected—!" the blond *cantinère* interrupted.

"This is no time to quarrel with each other," Belle pointed out. "Unless something is done, *madame la générale,* her husband and the Austrian will betray your country and may even bring about the defeat of your Army in Mexico."

"Madame la générale!" Alice blazed, going on to describe the blonde's ancestry in obscene detail.

"I'll scratch her eyes out!" Marthe declared furiously. "I'll tear her bald-headed and have her heart with my bare hands!"

There could be no doubting the sincerity with which the two women spoke. During her stay at the fort, Belle had come to know the two *cantinières* well enough for her to be able to read their emotions correctly.

"She'd have you shot if you tried," Belle warned Marthe, cutting across the women's tirades. "If you will do as I suggest, you might still save the situation."

"How?" Marthe inquired, and Alice stopped speaking to listen attentively.

"Can either of you ride?" Belle asked.

"I can," Alice admitted.

"You know that the old one, Rache, left the fort this afternoon?"

"Oui, mon colonel."

"He is waiting along the river," Belle explained, blessing the forethought that had caused the old-timer to ask for two horses so that he could ride relay and make better speed if he had to come back in a hurry. "If you can find some way of joining him, he will take you after Major de Redon's column and you can explain what is happening here."

"What *is* happening, *mon colonel*?" Marthe said.

Naturally the *cantinières* had been interested in the continued presence of the *bandido* gang contingents and not entirely satisfied with the official explanation that they had come to be hired to fight against the *Juáristas*. Such was the respect which Belle had built up, that the women accepted her explanation of how she had become involved in the affair. According to Belle, she had come, like many Confederate supporters, to offer her services to the French. The arrival of two Yankee enemies, along with other details, had combined to arouse her suspicions. So she and her Texas companions had played along with Caillard, learned what he planned to do and set about devising ways of circumventing him.

"You have done well, *mon colonel*," praised Marthe. "I will help you."

"And me," Alice promised. "But leaving the fort will not be easy. *Madame la générale* has ordered that nobody is let through the gates and the guards will obey."

"As long as they can," Belle agreed. "Have you wine?"

"Yes," Marthe confirmed. "But not enough to make the men drunk."

"I've something that will make them *sleep,*" Belle said. "It won't harm them, and by morning they will be awake. I think that when they learn the situation, the men will change their minds about deserting."

"It could go badly for you when the column returns, *mon colonel,*" Marthe warned. "Perhaps you should get away tonight."

"I mean to," Belle assured her. *"Cabrito* will saddle our horses and, as soon as the way is clear, we will leave. Before we go, we will help you arrest *madame la générale* and the Austrian. With them locked up, the others will make no trouble."

"If they try, I think we can persuade *madame* to talk them out of it," Alice said grimly. "A knife against her pretty face will do that."

Having decided upon cooperation, the *cantinières* put themselves wholeheartedly at Belle's disposal. Sending Alice to collect the Mexican girls, Belle asked Marthe to help her pack.

Before the first trunk had been filled and fastened, Belle heard the call of a whippoorwill outside her window. Only the fact that that particular bird was not found in Mexico told Belle some other agency had given the call. Going to the window, she looked down. The Ysabel Kid had completed his preparations at the stables and stood below, awaiting further orders.

"Where's *madame la générale,* Marthe?" Belle inquired.

"With the Austrian," the *cantinière* replied. "Probably sharing his bed."

Although Belle felt that the hour was too early for the latter possibility, she knew von Bulow's quarters faced the front of the building. So there seemed little likelihood of her being overheard by Sylvie. For all that, she pitched her voice as low as possible as she addressed the young Texan.

"They're with us, Lon. Wait until Alice comes out, then see her on her way. As soon as she's safe, we'll move out."

"Yo!" drawled the Kid, giving the traditional cavalry response. "I'll do that easy enough."

"Marthe and I will get my packs to the stable," Belle went on.

"Hosses're saddled up and ready to go," the Kid assured her. "I'll be around ready for her."

Assembling the *cantinières* in the passage, Alice confirmed that von Bulow was entertaining Sylvie in his quarters. Bringing the kegs in one at a time, so that the Mexican girls did not know what happened to them, Alice watched Belle give each a dose of a sleeping powder. Produced by Confederate chemists during the war, the powder had been of use to Belle on other occasions. Quick-acting, it left the recipient with a bad headache but had no serious effect. With the additions made, the girls were sent to present wine to the depleted garrison. Alice told the Mexican *cantinières* to include the men on guard at the gates or patrolling the terrepleins in the issue.

After the girls had departed, Marthe and Alice helped Belle to complete her packing. Having worn it since the day following the fight, Belle retained her uniform. She wondered if she should wear her gun belt, but decided against doing so. Changing her clothes or armament might arouse unwanted interest and comment. So she put the belt and Dance into her second trunk.

"We'll take them to the stables for you, Colonel," Marthe offered as Belle turned the key in the trunk's lock.

"Can you do it without being seen?"

"Yes. If we go down the back stairs and across the parade ground."

"Then do it," Belle said. "Let Alice get out of the fort, Marthe, then ask *Cabrito* to meet me in the main hall."

Fortunately the Frenchwomen had well-developed muscles, for Belle's two packsaddle trunks were not light. Watching them being carried off, Belle breathed a sigh of relief. Maybe Marthe and Alice would have raised no objections to what she intended to do next, but the girl wished to avoid letting them know about it. Belle was going to search Caillard's office in the hope of finding documentary evidence of the plot. If she could do so, it would be of the greatest use. Not only would such proof prevent a repetition of the scheme and prove the innocence of the United States Congress, it would remove the soft-shells who had originated it from their influential positions.

Belle did not hear any alarm raised, warning her that Alice and Marthe had been detected, as she descended to the small reception hall. Entering it, she found the hall illuminated in the usual way. A single chandelier hung from the center of the roof, the rope for raising or lowering it passing across and down to a hook in the wall alongside the door to Caillard's office.

Crossing to the office, Belle glanced toward the unlit mess hall. She tried the handle and the door opened to her push. Much to her surprise, she found that the office's lamp had been lit. Stepping inside, she decided that it had been done as a matter of routine. Or, maybe, Sylvie had been down to fetch something and not troubled to turn out the lamp on leaving. Whatever the reason, it would simplify Belle's search. Closing the door behind her, she stepped inside.

An examination of the desk's drawers yielded nothing. Not that she really expected to find incriminating papers in such a vulnerable location. Closing the last of the drawers, she went across to the safe in the corner of the room. One glance warned her that if the papers were inside, she had little chance of reaching them.

More in hope than expectancy, she tested the handle. A low hiss broke from her lips as it moved. Quickly Belle manipulated the handle and drew open the heavy door. Dropping to her left knee, she reached in and lifted up some of the papers.

At first, she felt that the reason the safe had not been locked was because it contained nothing of value. The documents inside might be of a confidential nature, but were only to do with the organization and running of the fort. Perhaps a supporter of the *Juárista* cause could have found use for them, yet Belle regarded the papers as of no importance. About to close the safe, she noticed a sabretache on the bottom shelf. Picking it up, she raised its flap and took out a sheet of paper. As she started to read her find, she knew that she had hit pay dirt.

Then she heard the door open and somebody step inside!

Turning her head, still kneeling, Belle saw Sylvie had entered. Although clad in her Hessian boots and scarlet breeches, she did not wear her tunic. Open considerably lower than convention and modesty accepted, her white silk blouse clung like a second skin, with nothing separating it from her white flesh. In her right hand, she held the rapier.

"We didn't like your *cantinière*'s drink, Boyd," Sylvie spat and kicked the door closed.

"Perhaps the rest of the garrison found them more acceptable," Belle replied.

"You'll not live to find out!" Sylvie warned and sprang across the room.

Thrusting herself erect, Belle hurled the sabretache toward Sylvie's face. Twisting aside, Sylvie interposed her sword-filled fist between her head and the missile. Belle watched the blonde knock the sabretache aside as she leapt away from the safe. Down and across flashed the girl's right hand, finding the hilt of her rapier and sliding the blade from its sheath. Releasing the paper, she sent her left hand flying to her belt's buckle. Immediately after the point emerged from the sheath, she set free and cast aside the belt.

The girl did not act an instant too soon. Already Sylvie had evaded the sabretache and commenced another assault. Around lashed the rapier's blade in a savage cut to the flank more suited to a saber than to the weapon she held. Suitable or not, the blow would have inflicted a near-fatal wound had it landed. Throwing herself to the rear, Belle passed beyond the arc of the blonde's blade. She missed being ripped open by inches, caught her balance and rapidly adopted the on guard stance best suited to the sword in her hand.

About to follow Belle for another try, Sylvie read the danger signs. Any further such wild attempts might easily prove fatal to the blonde. The Rebel Spy had recovered from her surprise, gained sufficient time to arm herself, and now stood ready to fight back. Having seen Belle in action at the *salle d'armes,* Sylvie was all too well aware of the other's ability. Only an objection to the chance of being seen at a disadvantage, however, had prevented Sylvie from crossing swords with Belle in mere competition. Faced with serious stakes, the blonde did not hesitate. Married to a poor, undistinguished French general, Sylvie had seen a chance of obtaining riches, either through her husband or von Bulow. The slender American girl threatened her chances. If Belle escaped with that damning paper, Sylvie would lose her opportunity—and maybe even her life.

16
DOUSE THE LIGHTS, BELLE

Balancing herself gracefully in the on guard position, Belle studied the blonde. Everything the girl saw warned her that she faced an opponent of considerable ability.

While the weapons they held were generally called rapiers, *épée de combat* would have been a more correct name. Shorter and lighter than the traditional rapier, each sword had a bell-shaped *coquille* guard, but no knuckle-bow on the hilt. Ending in a needlelike thrusting point, the triangular, fluted blade carried razor-sharp edges to permit the use of a slash or cut. Handling them required a special technique which Sylvie had clearly mastered.

Raising her left hand level with her head, the blonde turned her torso sideways to Belle. Sylvie stood pointing her slightly bent right leg in the girl's direction and turned her left foot outward. Held in a near classic well-covered *sixte* with a low point, the *coquille* shielded her sword hand, wrist and forearm in a position ideally suited to offense or defense. However, Sylvie used neither for a moment. Instead, she flicked a glance toward the safe.

"I've told Gautier so many times about forgetting to lock that door," the blonde hissed angrily. "He always was a fool."

"That shows in his choice of a wife," Belle answered.

Fury twisted at Sylvie's face and she attacked. Their blades met, in a rapid hissing clash of steel, feeling out the other's potential. For all her anger, the blonde refused to be led into rashness. The first passes were in the nature of a *sentiment du fer,* feeling the opponent's reactions through the contact of the blades. Nothing in that exchange caused Belle to revise her opinion of Sylvie's skill, nor the blonde to decide she had overestimated the girl.

Belle feinted low and Sylvie accepted the bait, trying for a stop hit. Deftly Belle parried it by *sixte* and went into a straight thrust. Despite its swift and capable conception, the girl's second-intention attack failed to reach flesh. Again Sylvie parried and began a *prise-de-fer,* taking Belle's blade on her own to carry it in a circle ready for the delivery of a thrust. Apparently yielding, Belle allowed her blade to be rotated. By bending her arm and raising her point at the completion of the rotation, Belle brought off a well-timed parry in *quarte.* She followed it with a swift riposte that caused the blonde to make a rapid leap to the rear.

Hissing through her teeth like an enraged cobra, Sylvie launched a savage *flèche.* Almost running to the attack, she forced Belle to retreat. Changing from pure *épée* fighting, the blonde whipped around a vicious cut toward Belle's head. Going below Sylvie's blade in a graceful, effective *passata sotto* evasion, Belle sent her point leaping toward the tight-stretched, pulsating front of the white silk blouse. Twisting aside, Sylvie felt a needle-prick sensation against her ribs. The silk split as the Rebel Spy's blade grazed her flesh.

Cutting back as she turned, Sylvie's sword slit through the shoulder of Belle's tunic. Delivered from almost out of range, only the point and last two inches of the foible* made the con-

---

* *Foible:* half of the blade nearest to the point.

tact. Like Sylvie, Belle had received a scratch that would not seriously incapacitate her.

Certainly neither showed any sign of flinching or hesitation. Facing each other, they met in a rapid exchange which took them twice across the room. The engagement halted when Sylvie performed a parry of *septime* and turned both blades upward. Sliding together, the *coquilles* brought the move to a halt with the opponents almost breast to breast. For a good twenty seconds they remained locked *corps à corps,* using strength in an attempt to bring about a separation. The blonde's voluptuous body had an advantage of weight that counteracted the steel-spring power of the girl's slender frame. So much so that it seemed that they had reached a stalemate. Sweat trickled down their faces. Each girl tried to push the other off balance, escape and make the most of the advantage she gained.

Suddenly Sylvie brought down her left hand, bunching it into a fist that drove for Belle's stomach. Just in time, the girl braced herself. Grunting in pain as the blow landed, she reeled to the rear. With a spat-out, triumphant curse, the blonde leapt and cut for Belle's head. Again a *passata sotto* saved Belle from injury. However, she not only went under the blade, but thrust herself to the left. Snapping a side kick in passing, Belle spiked the heel of her right boot into the top of Sylvie's thigh. Changing from triumph to pain, Sylvie's voice faded as she stumbled against the wall.

For all that, the blonde had returned to the on guard position before Belle could reach her. Approaching Sylvie, the girl changed her style of attack and handled her sword as if it was a saber. Partially taken by surprise, the blonde also changed style to match her assailant's. Clearly Belle had a slight, yet significant edge in a cut-and-thrust engagement. Enough to make Sylvie put up a defensive box for her protection, guarding the vertical lines of her magnificent torso and from above the top of her head to below the waist. It was a blockade through which nothing could break—but expensive in energy. Sweat soaked the blonde's face and caused her blouse to cling in an even more revealing manner to her body. Her hair, let down in preparation for a love-making session with von Bulow, straggled untidily and wetly.

Back and forward the fight raged across the office, with neither girl gaining a definite advantage nor scoring further hits. Both had come very close. A lunge by Belle had torn Sylvie's left sleeve from wrist to armpit without touching flesh. Later, only a leap to the rear had saved Belle from worse damage than that caused by a cut opening up the front of her tunic.

Reaching the center of the room, they again attained a state of *corps à corps*. Recalling Sylvie's last escape from the position, Belle prepared to deal with a similar attempt. This was no friendly—or rivalry-induced—competition. Nor could it be classed as a formal duel. It was a fight to the death in which all thoughts of fair play could be forgotten. Seeing the blonde knot her left fist, Belle kicked her hard on the front of her right shin. Sylvie let out a squeal, falling back a little. Bringing down her own left hand, Belle laid it against the perspiration-soddened bosom of Sylvie's blouse. Combining the thrust of her left arm with the pressure already being exerted against the blonde's sword, Belle hurled Sylvie from her. Going backward, Sylvie collided with the desk. Unable to stop herself, the blonde went over the top. The sword flew from her hand, clattering to the floor in the corner of the room. Then the woman fell from Belle's sight beyond the desk.

Driven back a few short steps by the force she had applied to pushing Sylvie away, Belle caught her balance. What she saw sent her bounding toward the desk. In falling, Sylvie had landed kneeling and twisted in the girl's direction. Down went Sylvie's right hand, entering her breeches' pocket and emerging holding a four-barreled Sharps Triumph metal-cartridge pistol.

At the first hint that the blonde had another weapon, Belle forced herself into motion. Reaching the desk, she hurled herself across it. Still kneeling, the blonde began to raise the little hide-out pistol and thumb back its hammer. With the quadruple muzzles, looking far greater than their actual .32 caliber, lifting to point at her, Belle glided over the desk on her stomach. Held ahead of her, the blade of Belle's sword reached the blonde. Perforating the top of Sylvie's left breast, the point of Belle's sword continued its downward and rearward advance. Driven on by the girl's weight, the sword spiked through its recipient's heart.

Sudden, violent agony ripped through Sylvie, preventing her from keeping the pistol aimed at Belle. Jerking uncontrollably, the little weapon tilted upward at the instant its user involuntarily pressed on the exposed, guardless trigger. Belle heard the crack of the shot, felt the muzzle blast lightly on her face, then she collided with Sylvie and they both crashed to the floor. Belle felt the sword's hilt torn from her grasp and saw the Sharps spin out of the blonde's hand. Rolling clear, the girl snatched up the little pistol. Twisting into a sitting position, Belle swung her feet around until she was facing Sylvie. Impaled by the sword, the blonde sprawled upon her back. Even as Belle watched, holding the Sharps ready for use, *madame la générale*'s body gave a final convulsive shudder and slumped limply, with hands falling from the blade of the girl's sword. A low gasping sigh of satisfaction broke from Belle. The murders of Eve Coniston and the Mexican *cantinière* had been avenged and repaid in full.

Taking a few seconds to recover her breath, Belle stood up. She lowered the Sharps' hammer to half cock and dropped it into her own breeches' pocket. Reaching over with her right hand, Belle touched the gash in her tunic's left shoulder. Under the separated edges of cloth, she found a shallow groove in her flesh. It was still bleeding a little, but she knew that the wound was not serious.

Going to the blonde's body, Belle retrieved her sword. The girl experienced no remorse or regret at killing Sylvie. There lay a ruthless, cold-hearted woman who had used the attributes of sex so generously provided by nature to ensnare and delude men. Sylvie had been willing to kill to gain her ends and had met the fate she deserved.

About to leave the office, Belle saw the discarded sheet of paper. Crossing, she picked it up. In her hands, she held Caillard's orders. Clearly the general did not trust his superiors, for he had insisted on the whole scheme being outlined and signed by Maximilian's second-in-command. So the girl possessed evidence of the plot. Unfortunately it did not name the accomplices from the United States, other than Tollinger and Barmain.

"It's better than nothing, though," Belle told herself, as she folded the paper and slipped it into the inside breast pocket of her tunic.

Ignoring the dead woman, Belle collected and buckled on her belt. Keeping the sword unsheathed, she went to the door. Even as she stepped out, she wondered where von Bulow was—and very rapidly discovered the answer.

Along the hall, the Kid came through the rear door. At the same moment, von Bulow and four of his men appeared out of the darkened mess hall. By sheer reflex action, Belle emerged from Caillard's office and closed its door, which proved a mighty fortunate action. All the men held revolvers, while von Bulow carried his saber in addition to the handgun. The Kid reacted first and fastest to the unexpected multiple confrontation.

"Douse the lights, Belle!" the youngster roared, throwing his Dragoon into an instinctive alignment on what he hoped would be von Bulow.

Touching off the shot, the Kid hoped that Belle would show her usual effective grasp of the situation and rapid response to it. Caught in the chest, the man at von Bulow's right screamed and pitched backward into the mess hall. The shriek sounded so loud and unexpectedly that the other men—all Austrians—froze on hearing it. Taking her chance, Belle lashed around with her sword. Striking the rope, the blade sliced through and the chandelier plunged down. Impacting against the floor, its candles were extinguished and the hall plunged into darkness.

Just before the blackness descended, Belle saw the Kid fling himself toward the center of the room. Instinctively the girl thrust herself rearward, to pass before the door of Caillard's office in her companion's direction. Four shots roared from von

Bulow's party. Belle heard the deep "whomp!" of lead striking the wall behind her. Only one bullet came, the others having been aimed at the young Texan's recently vacated position.

"Get down and lie still, Belle!" ordered the Kid's voice, coming with an almost ventriloquial quality that made pinpointing its location difficult.

Obediently, without thought of objecting, Belle prepared to obey. They were playing the Kid's kind of a game: a deadly version of blindman's bluff in which a single whisper, a loud breath or an incautious movement could be fatal.

Another shot bellowed from across the corridor. Its muzzle blast momentarily flared bright enough to illuminate all von Bulow's party except for the wounded man. He made his presence felt by groaning piteously. No answer left the Kid's old Dragoon. After the brief glow of light had gone, a hurried scuffling of feet warned the listening girl and Texan that the Austrians had split up as soon as the darkness returned to shield their movements.

With infinite care, Belle grasped the sheath of her sword. Feeling about her with it, she moved so slowly that even if the steel-tipped case had struck the wall or the floor, it would not have raised a warning sound. Equally carefully, she lowered herself into a prone position. Reaching out with the toe of her right boot, she touched the wall. Showing even greater caution, she laid down her sword and extended its free hand to feel at the jamb on the hinges side of the door. Having established her location, she crept silent fingers over the floor until she regained possession of the rapier's hilt. Armed and recumbent, she listened, waiting to hear anything to tell her how she might best help the Kid.

Each succeeding moan from the stricken soldier decreased in volume, until he lapsed into unconsciousness. Then a deep, utter silence closed over the hall, one that seemed charged with electric menace.

Taking advantage of the noise made by the injured man, the Kid had advanced to the center of the hall. In his right hand, he held the cocked Dragoon Colt. Almost without the need for conscious direction, his left hand had produced and now gripped the bowie knife. When the sounds ended, he stopped and his ears started to pick up other faint noises previously smothered by the groaning. The Kid stood like a statue; except that no statue had ever possessed such latent, deadly preparedness. Nor was a cougar, crouched upon a limb above a deer trail, more alert, wary or ready for instant action than the Kid.

"Come on, you stinking Austrian *pelados*!" thought the Kid. "Make some more noise, 'n' right now, blast you."

Unfortunately, the Austrians proved unreceptive to thought suggestions. Instead, they continued to keep quiet. Not that they remained motionless. Displaying a skill at silent movement that the Kid found hard to credit to members of a European army, von Bulow and his remaining men advanced stealthily through the darkness. The Kid could hear them, but not sufficiently well to permit him to shoot with any hope of making a hit. So he did not try. To cut loose under the prevailing conditions offered too good an indication of one's whereabouts to be contemplated.

Seconds ticked by, or dragged away on leaden, crawling feet, and Belle guessed at the reason for the Kid's inactivity. She also wondered how she might be of use. It was not in the nature of the Rebel Spy to crouch passively in the dark and let a friend take all the risks. Rising and moving around did not provide an acceptable answer. Yet something had to be done. Perhaps the *cantinières* had failed to deliver the drugged drinks to the garrison. If so, men carrying lamps or lanterns would soon converge on the main building. Once the hall was illuminated again, Belle and the Kid could count their life expectancy in seconds. Von Bulow would show them no mercy.

Something hard dug into the girl's thigh and after a moment she realized what it was. Setting down her sword, she eased the little Sharps Triumph pistol from her breeches' pocket. Hardly daring to breathe, she inched the hammer to full cock. Nobody gave any indication of hearing the faint click. Making sure that she did not touch the rapier, she eased her torso upward a little. Supporting herself on her left forearm, she hurled the Sharps so that it would strike the wall some distance away and above her. She did not know if the pistol carried a full load, but hoped that it did. Already the upper right barrel had been discharged in Caillard's office. Given luck, the remaining three tubes each held a cartridge.

Even if the gun did not go off, Belle hoped that the clatter of its arrival against the wall might bring about the desired result. Not until the Sharps had left her hand did she realize that the Kid would not know who had thrown it. However, she hoped that he would make the correct assumption and act accordingly.

Turning in its flight, the bottom of the pistol struck the stone of the wall. The Sharps Triumph did not have a guard around its trigger, an omission noted for a lack of safety. Slammed back by the impact, the trigger set the hammer free. Rotated by the action of the hammer being taken to full cock, the striker slammed against the base of the cartridge in the upper left barrel. Flame spurted and powder's gas ejected the bullet at roughly the height a man might hold the pistol when shooting.

Four guns roared from scattered points in the blackness, echoed by a fifth. From her place on the floor, Belle could tell that the first quartet had been aimed toward where her pistol had detonated. The fifth man had fired in the direction of the shooter nearest to him. Due to the ringing, confused, ear-shattering concussion of the gunplay, Belle could not decide which type of revolver had fired which shot. Anxiety gnawed at her as she wondered if the Kid might have become a victim of her trick.

Hearing the faint clink caused by the Sharps striking against the wall, the Kid started to turn his Dragoon that way. When he saw the comparatively minute jet of flame, and considered the noise made by the light powder charge erupting, he knew that they did not originate from the revolvers of his enemies. Yet, to the best of his knowledge, Belle did not own a firearm capable of producing the sound.

If one of the Austrians had tried to trick the Kid into revealing his position, the scheme was backfiring. Automatically, the youngster noted the places from which the shots roared. One in front of the door to the mess hall; most likely fired by von Bulow, who was letting his men take the chances of stalking the two Americans. Two, down to the other end of the hall. Three, over in the center of the floor and about level with Caillard's door. Which left number four.

He stood not six feet from the Kid!

There was one European who possessed a real quiet set of feet. Likely his other senses were not equal to the softness with which he moved. Clearly he was unaware of the Kid's proximity to him. He learned soon enough, but the knowledge came too late to be of use.

Up swung the Dragoon, lining on the spot from which the muzzle blast had glowed. Pressing the trigger, the Kid sent a bullet on its way and flung himself aside. He heard the unmistakable sound of a round lead ball driving through a human chest cavity. Losing all his earlier silence of movement, the stricken man blundered back a few steps before crashing to the floor.

Only three shots came in answer to the Kid's Dragoon. Directed to the spot from which he had fired, none of the bullets came anywhere near him. Although he had cocked his revolver on its recoil, the young Texan refrained from attempting to down another of his assailants.

"Colonel Boyd!" called von Bulow, confirming the Kid's guess as to his position. "I suppose *Madame* Caillard is dead."

"Right where I figured you to be!" breathed the Kid, pleased that Belle did not reply. "Keep talking, soldier boy, and you're right soon going to wish you hadn't."

"Come now, Colonel Boyd," the Austrian obliged. "Sylvie came down to her husband's office to make sure that he had left the safe door locked. She must have found you there and, as you came out, I assume that she cannot. I believe a change of command is in order for our little enterprise. Two colonels are better than one inefficient general."

Silently as a snake crossing soft grass, the Kid glided in the speaker's direction. All the time the youngster was advancing, moving slowly, he kept all his Indian-keen senses at work. His every instinct warned him that something was wrong. At first he could not imagine what it might be.

Then the realization struck home and brought him to a halt, ears, eyes and even nostrils working with increased care. Nothing the Kid had seen about von Bulow led him to like the Austrian, but he could not honestly claim he believed the other to be stupid or incompetent. A man with von Bulow's training and knowledge of warfare did not endanger himself by giving away his location unless he had a valid reason to do so. Certainly the Austrian did not intend keeping to the offer he was making. Nor would he expect Belle to accept it.

"Come on, Colonel Boyd!" von Bulow continued and the Kid resumed his ghostlike approach. "We can carry out this plan without the help of the Caillards."

By that time the Kid had come close to the place from which the voice originated. Estimating how far he had moved, the youngster knew he was close to the connecting door to the mess hall. Two more strides, three at most, ought to bring him into contact with von Bulow. With their leader dead or captured, the other Austrians might be induced to give up the fight.

Tensing to launch his final attack, the Kid heard a creaking of hinges. The door to Caillard's office began to open. Light flooded across the small rear hall, illuminating the Kid. It also showed him von Bulow, standing partially concealed on the other side of the mess-hall's entrance.

Listening to von Bulow, Belle almost mirrored the Kid's train of thought. Aware that von Bulow did not make the offer with an expectancy of acceptance, she wondered what his motivation might be. Then she heard a faint sound, barely audible above the Austrian's voice, very close ahead.

A man was approaching Belle's position, feeling his way along the wall; which raised a point. Who was it? The Kid—or one of the Austrians? Knowing the dark youngster's ability at silent movement, Belle doubted if it would be the former. Which meant the man must be an enemy, probably searching for her.

Displaying the same caution that she had shown in all her movements since the chandelier had fallen, Belle unbuckled her belt and removed it. Then she eased herself upward until she assumed a posture almost like that adopted by a sprinter awaiting the signal to start the race. The faint sounds before her came to a halt and Belle froze. Had the man located her? Bringing up her sword, she extended its point in the direction she figured him to be.

Just an instant too late, the girl became aware of what her neighbor was planning to do. The door of Caillard's office opened and, before the glow of light dazzled her, Belle saw that von Bulow's burly sergeant was gripping its handle. Either von Bulow had signaled instructions in some way, or the sergeant had shown a shrewd grasp of the tactical situation. Under cover of his colonel's words, the man had crept across the room. Reaching the wall, he had felt his way along it, found and pushed to open the door.

Not that Belle wasted time considering the sergeant's motivation. By good luck, she was crouching in the darkness beyond the door's light. Either the sergeant was half blinded by the glare, or concentrating his attention on locating the Kid, for he did not look the girl's way. Driving herself forward, Belle heard the soldier's startled curse. Then she lunged and her blade passed between his ribs. Pain and surprise caused him to rock backward and release the door's handle. Discarding the rapier's hilt as she felt its point driving home, Belle grabbed for the handle and jerked the door closed to cut off the light which endangered the Kid. Guns thundered as Belle completed her work and flung herself away from the door.

Fast as Belle moved, the effort would have been wasted but for the lightning speed of the Kid's reactions. An expression of shock came to von Bulow's face as he discovered how close the young Texan had come to him. Bringing up his Army Colt as he lunged through the mess hall door, the Austrian fired. So did the last of the soldiers, sighting and turning lead loose with commendable speed if not accuracy.

Flinging himself out of the lighted area, the Kid felt a burning sensation across his right forearm. Pain caused him to open his fingers and drop the Dragoon. Cursing von Bulow's lucky shot, the Kid propelled himself toward the shadows beyond the cone of light. Another bullet passed over his head. Then Belle had dealt with the sergeant and closed the door to bring back a darkened state to the hall.

Feet pounded as von Bulow's remaining man ran along the hall toward where he had last seen the Kid. That, as anybody along the bloody border could have told the man, was no way to tangle with *Cuchillo,* grandson of Long Walker. Shaking his stinging right arm, the Kid satisfied himself that it still worked. While in pain, he had suffered no more than a graze.

"I allus said shaped bullets're no good," the Kid mused as he transferred the knife to his right hand.

Guided by his ears, the Kid went to meet the soldier. Blundering on through stygian gloom, the man kicked his foot against the chandelier. At the same moment, he felt something strike his stomach and sudden, shocking, numbing pain blasted into him. Doubling over, he let his revolver clatter to the floor. His hands clawed at the terrible gash torn into his lower body. Crumpling to his knees, he fell forward onto his face.

"A:he" grunted the Kid. He had delivered a savage, raking chop with his bowie knife, showing the same deadly aim as when he could see his target.

Hearing the commotion, von Bulow took a chance. He sighed and fired toward it, hoping for a hit or a sight of his enemy in the muzzle's flash. Although the latter materialized, the former failed. The red glow illuminated the Kid, and the last of the soldiers tumbling to the floor with blood gushing from his slit-open stomach. Leaping clear of the dying man, the Kid heard and saw another chamber of von Bulow's Colt emptied. Its discharged bullet came nowhere near the youngster and he had avoided the glare of the muzzle blast.

"You all right, Belle?" called the Kid, sounding almost at von Bulow's left elbow.

Twisting around, the Austrian restrained his first impulse to squeeze the Colt's trigger. A scuffling sound came from his right, causing him to swivel rapidly in that direction. Still he refused to shoot.

"I'm fine, Lon," Belle answered. "How about you, Otto?"

"He's sweating, Belle," the Kid declared. "I can smell it on him."

Von Bulow became uneasily aware of the sweat that ran down his face. His clothing seemed wet with it and he wondered if the Kid could smell it. Slowly, a step at a time, the Austrian eased himself toward the mess hall's wall. If he could get that at his back, he would be comparatively safe until help came—

What help?

Clearly the other *cantinières* had been more successful than the one who had visited his men. She had failed because the Austrian cared little for wine and the sergeant possessed a suspicious nature. Forcing the girl to drink from her keg, he had observed the results and reported his findings to the colonel. Aware of what kind of men Caillard had attracted to his cause, von Bulow doubted if any—even those on duty—would have refused to drink. So the whole revolutionary garrison was probably lying in a drugged sleep.

For the first time in his life, von Bulow must stand or fall by his own efforts. He must—

A savage screech shattered the silence!

It came from very close. So close, in fact, that von Bulow could not prevent himself firing the Colt. To the extreme edge of the muzzle-glow, he saw a fast moving figure. Such was the savagery of its features that he could not resist cocking the Colt and pressing the trigger. Only a click rewarded his action.

"Your gun's empty, Count von Bulow," Belle called. "Throw it down and surrender."

"To a woman and a half-breed?" the Austrian answered, letting the Colt drop and taking the saber in his right hand. "Never!"

With that, he raised the saber and commenced to move it in a defensive box before him. If that damned young Texan came too close, he would meet with a length of cold steel far in excess to that of his bowie knife.

Somebody entered the hall, carrying a lantern that threw a cloud of light through the blackness. In it, von Bulow saw the young Texan ahead of him. With a bellow of mixed rage and triumph, the Austrian sprang and lashed a blow intended to take the Kid's head from the black-clad shoulders. Expecting no trouble in dealing with the Indian-dark youngster, von Bulow received a rapid disillusionment.

Throwing himself forward and down before his attacker, the Kid let the blade pass over his head. He struck upward, slicing the bowie's blade through the inside of von Bulow's left thigh. Blood burst from the femoral artery and the great saphenous vein as the knife severed them. Bringing his blade free, the Kid twisted himself over and rolled along the floor clear of von Bulow's down-swinging saber. Before he could strike again, the Austrian staggered and crashed forward in a faint induced by a rapid loss of blood. Thirty seconds later, he was dead.

"Colonel Boyd!" Marthe croaked from behind the lantern. "Are you all right? Did I come soon enough?"

"You almost came too soon," Belle replied, standing up and walking across to the Kid.

17
WE CAN USE YOU,
COLONEL BOYD

"After that, leaving the fort was easy," Belle told General Philo Handiman, repeating the story of her exploits in Mexico some six weeks after they had ended. "All Caillard's men had been drugged, so Lon Ysabel and I had our injuries treated and rode out before midnight. Rache caught up with us near Matamoros and said that Major de Redon had accepted the *cantinière*'s story, then turned straight back. De Redon sent his cavalry screen ahead and Rache had been close by to see what happened. They reached the fort and were admitted, either by the garrison or the *cantinières*. So the French are still in possession of it and can't even blame the United States for its loss."

Big, heavily built, capable-looking, Handiman was in uniform. He looked at the slender, beautiful girl who sat erect on a chair in the sitting room of his suite at Bannister's Hotel. Nodding his head, he signified his approval. It seemed that the Rebel Spy had performed a dangerous task and very thoroughly ruined a plan that might have involved the United States in another costly war.

Despite the hectic nature of her last visit, the hotel's manager had not recognized Belle when she had taken a room under his roof. On her arrival in Brownsville, the girl had visited the address given to her by Eve Coniston. Being granted an interview on sending in Eve's password, Belle had given a full account of the happenings at Fort Mendez to a U.S. Army colonel. Requesting that the girl should stay in town, he had passed the information with all speed to his superior in Washington. To avoid attracting attention, Belle had become a blonde, dressing and acting the part of a young officer's wife waiting to join him at his regiment along the Rio Grande.

"The time wasn't wasted," Belle assured Handiman when he mentioned the matter. "The Ysabels and I spent it checking out a few things that had been troubling us, such as where Tollinger and Barmain hid in Matamoros."

"Where?" asked Handiman hopefully.

"With the French garrison. The last place we would have expected them to be, not knowing about the plot. It seems they didn't trust their hosts enough to mention me. Or it may have been that there were Southerners around."

"In which case, they wouldn't dare to make trouble for the Rebel Spy." Handiman grinned. "Unfortunately we've only your unsupported statement to use against Smethurst, and I'm afraid that wouldn't be enough. Wishing no disrespect to you."

"I understand." Belle smiled, pleased that she had an excuse not to mention one aspect of the affair.

Receiving the names of some of the intellectuals, Don Francisco Almonte had stated his satisfaction. Belle had not troubled to learn to what use he placed the knowledge gathered by her party.

"Did all your men escape?" Handiman inquired after a moment.

"All my *friends* escaped," Belle agreed. "Cactus slipped away from his party before they boarded the ship. Sam Ysabel deserted Caillard three days' ride from the fort. We haven't heard what happened to Caillard, but I should imagine he met with a warm reception on his return."

"Where are your friends now?" Handiman asked, accepting the rebuke implied by the girl's emphasis and correction.

"Rache and Cactus decided that they'd like a spell of quiet living and have gone to work on a friend's ranch in the San Garcia country.* The Ysabels planned to start mustanging again and left two weeks ago, when they felt sure that they could trust you Yankees enough for me to be safe in your hands."

Although Belle did not know it, the Ysabel family's plans had been changed. The discovery of a plot to assassinate Juárez had caused them to return to Mexico. Doing so would cost Sam Ysabel his life and send the Kid on a danger-filled hunt for revenge.†

"That's a pity," Handiman said. "We can use you, Colonel Boyd, and could have found employment for them. Will you join the U.S. Secret Service?"

Ever since her arrival in Brownsville, Belle had thought about how she would react if she received such an offer. Faced with it, she could not bring herself to make an immediate answer. Yet, at the bottom of her heart, she knew that there could only be one reply.

As she had told the sailors in the hotel's dining room, on the night of her meeting with the Ysabels, the war was over. Her experiences with Eve Coniston and the courtesy shown by the woman's superiors had reminded Belle that not all Yankees belonged to Tollinger and Barmain's breed. The Confederate States no longer existed. Nothing remained of Belle's prewar way of life. If it came to a point, she would find things too dull if she stopped being a spy. So she might just as well put her skills to use for the benefit of her reunited country.

"It will be a honor, General," Belle said sincerely.

Crossing the room, Handiman picked up a Bible on which the Rebel Spy could at last swear her allegiance to the United States.

---

* More of Cactus and Rache's story can be read in *McGraw's Inheritance*.
† How the Kid avenged his father and the effect doing so had upon his life is told in *The Ysabel Kid.*

J.T. EDSON

Brings to Life the Fierce and Often Bloody Struggles of the Untamed West

__ THE BAD BUNCH	20764-9	$3.50
__ THE FASTEST GUN IN TEXAS	20818-1	$3.50
__ NO FINGER ON THE TRIGGER	20749-5	$3.50
__ SLIP GUN	20772-X	$3.50
__ TROUBLED RANGE	20773-8	$3.50
__ JUSTICE OF COMPANY Z	20858-0	$3.50
__ McGRAW'S INHERITANCE	20869-6	$3.50
__ RAPIDO CLINT	20868-8	$3.50
__ COMMANCHE	20930-7	$3.50

FLOATING OUTFIT SERIES

__ THE HIDE AND TALLOW MEN	20862-9	$3.50
__ THE NIGHTHAWK	20726-6	$3.50